floodmarkers

FLOODMARKERS

Nic Brown

COUNTERPOINT

BERKELEY

This is a work of fiction. Names, characters, places, and
incidents are the product of the author's imagination or are
used fictitiously. Any resemblance to actual persons, living
or dead, is entirely coincidental.

"Trampoline" was published in *Glimmer Train*, "Steak"
(under the name "The Neighbor's Yard") appeared in the
South Carolina Review, "Libertee Meats" appeared in *Epoch*,
and "Quickening" was published in the *Harvard Review*.

Library of Congress Cataloging-in-Publication Data
Brown, Nic, 1977–
Floodmarkers / Nic Brown.
p. cm.
ISBN 978-1-58243-506-0
1. Hurricane Hugo, 1989—Fiction.
2. Community life—Fiction.
3. Life change events—Fiction.
4. North Carolina—Fiction. I. Title.
PS3602.R72242F58 2009   813'.6—dc22
2008051285

Cover design by Silverander Communications
Interior design by David Bullen
Printed in the United States of America

Counterpoint
2117 Fourth Street
Suite D
Berkeley, CA 94710

www.counterpointpress.com

Distributed by Publishers Group West

10 9 8 7 6 5 4 3 2 1

For

Abby Brown

Daniel Wallace

Matthew Vollmer

Kevin Moffett

Jonathan Ames

James Alan McPherson

Darren Jessee

and

Frances Brown

CONTENTS

BEFORE SUNRISE

*In Charleston right now, the wind will pick up any-
thing. It will pick up little rocks off the ground. It will
take things off your truck and make them missiles.
It's gusting over 110 miles an hour right now and they
haven't even seen the worst of it. What that means for
us at this hour is rain. Three and a half inches so far as
the first storm bands enter the viewing area.*

   *That's a view of downtown Raleigh, quiet at this
hour. Look at that. That should only increase, with
a good chance that winds could reach tropical storm,
even hurricane, strength here in the Piedmont by noon.
That's something, people, that we haven't seen in this
area since the records have been kept.*

   For more, let's go to the map.

dice

○ ○ ○ ○ ○ ○ ○ ○ ○

The lights were off but the glass door was unlocked and Cliff followed Matthew into the tanning salon. Inside, Cliff blinked rain out of his eyes as they adjusted to the dark. It was near 4:00 AM and the street lamps shone weakly through the windows onto two dusty plastic plants and a framed poster of the tropics.

It seemed like they should be quiet, but Matthew said, "I think she'll be here. This shit is insane."

Then he opened a door in the back of the room and light cut out of the space like every fluorescent bulb in Lystra had been turned on at once. Past the door, seven tanning beds were turned on and a naked body lay in each. Sausage legs led up to hairy crotches, and then more naked people were just sitting around on long, slatted wooden benches. Many had drinks in their hands.

"What the hell is this?" Cliff said.

"See. It's insane," Matthew said.

"They're all naked."

"*Yeah* they're all naked!" Matthew yelled, making Cliff jump.

A naked man yelled back, "We're all naked!" and people began to laugh. One of the bodies lying in a tanning bed wiggled its toes vigorously.

It was all Cliff could do not to turn and run back into the rain. But he didn't. Instead, he pulled at his damp suit jacket. He straightened his tie. And he scanned the room for Rebecca. She was not there.

Rebecca was the one getting married tomorrow. She was Cliff's first and only cousin and she lived here in Lystra. Cliff lived in Chattanooga and had never even been here before. From all indications, though, things in Lystra did not fit into Cliff's normal experience. First off, a hurricane—Hugo—was due to blow through in the morning. Secondly, Cliff was getting the sense that the social scene here was unlike that of his high school friends at home.

He had hoped to make it to the rehearsal dinner and had driven in that afternoon with his parents—seven and a half hours in the Town & Country station wagon, across the Appalachians and into North Carolina. Still, they'd gotten in late and missed almost everything. When Cliff and his parents walked into the hotel event room, there was only one very pale busboy cleaning up.

Cliff knew it was stupid, but he was devastated. He wanted Rebecca to see him in his new suit, to see that she wasn't the only one who had grown up and moved on. There was tomorrow, too, but he needed to capitalize on what time he had. After they checked into the Red Roof Inn, he called Matthew, Rebecca's ex-stepbrother, from the front desk. Matthew's father had divorced Rebecca's mother before Rebecca was born, but Matthew always seemed to be around. Every time Cliff had seen him he was either drunk or just embarrassing. Cliff felt sure he'd know where everyone had gone, and on the phone he said that he did and that he was going out anyway and that it was good to hear from him and that Lystra was a shit hole but it was his shit hole and Cliff should get ready to tear this shit hole up!

Cliff had never even been to a bar. He was only seventeen. But he had his own room at the Red Roof Inn and his parents didn't even know that he'd left. After three bars, though, Rebecca still was yet to be seen. That was when Matthew led the way to this place. According to him, Tanfastic had parties.

Standing there, looking at all the naked tanners, none of whom

dice

were Rebecca, Cliff felt both disappointed and relieved. He did want to find her, but he was also so nervous. It had been two years since he'd seen her.

▭ ▭ ▭

When Cliff was eight and Rebecca was nine, their families vacationed together in Myrtle Beach. It was the first of many trips there and Cliff and Rebecca shared a bedroom. On the third afternoon there, Cliff watched Rebecca take off her clothes as she prepared to put on her bathing suit. He wasn't hidden or anything; he just stood there watching her undress. She'd told him he could watch her if she could watch him. They were only kids, so they weren't thinking about the fact that they were cousins. When Cliff took his clothes off, Rebecca told him to slowly turn around three times. After that, Cliff asked her if she would lick his stomach. He didn't know how he thought of this, but she did it. She licked his stomach.

▭ ▭ ▭

There's a strange pressure being the only clothed person in a room, Cliff thought. He was sitting on a bench with a girl whom Matthew had just introduced him to. She was Rebecca's old roommate, but Cliff couldn't remember her name. She was young, around Rebecca's age, eighteen or so, tiny with short blond hair, the smallest breasts, a gap between her front teeth, large freckles that bridged from cheek to cheek, and no clothing on at all. Her soft round face was snorting cocaine off of a *People* magazine that lay in the lap of a man who was naked, too, though the magazine in his lap covered things up. Leona Helmsley was on the cover. After the girl was done, she wiped white dust off of Leona's forehead with her index finger.

"Oh yeah, Rebecca's coming," she said, rubbing her gums with the finger. "For sure." She put the magazine in her own lap. "You want some?" She held up a rolled dollar bill.

"Is it cocaine?"

"We put in some of my Ritalin, too."

"Oh." This made no sense to Cliff. "No, thanks. That's OK."

"OK, but if you want, it's not that big a deal."

Cliff looked at her stomach and thought he would do anything this girl ever asked of him. And, he thought, what was he going to look like if he just sat there doing nothing? What if Rebecca came in and saw him like that—just sitting there?

"OK," Cliff said.

She gave him the one-dollar tube and he lowered his face to her lap. His head brushed her stomach as he quickly inhaled the powder off of Leona.

Afterwards, Cliff said, "Whoa. I think I'm just drunk and hyper and happy."

"Me too you should take your clothes off."

"What?"

"Me too you should take your clothes off."

Cliff's new suit was too large for him and had a purple handkerchief sewn into the jacket pocket. At first Cliff thought it was nice, and he had hoped that Rebecca would get a good look at him in it, but now it was making him self-conscious. People kept saying, "Nice handkerchief."

There was an older man with a huge grey beard beside them who had just taken off a pair of overalls. His body had the appearance of an old hide that had been poorly skinned, then stretched over a rocking chair to dry, and on his back he had a tattoo of a dancing rabbit from which several coarse white hairs grew. Nobody was even looking at him.

"Come on," the girl said.

dice

So Cliff took his suit off. He folded the pants and jacket and set them on the edge of the bench, and when it got to his underwear, he pulled it off quickly, like diving into a pool to quicken the shock.

"You want to tan with me?" the girl said.

"Yeah. But actually no. I burn easily."

"At a tanning salon," she said, "they control the amount of UV so that you don't burn. Whatever your skin type."

⊂ ⊂ ⊂

When Cliff was fifteen and Rebecca sixteen—this was two summers earlier—they returned to Myrtle Beach. It was the last trip they all took together.

By the second night, Cliff was already sunburnt from only a couple hours in the water. The itch and throb of his red flesh kept him awake, aching and stinging at each toss and turn. He got out of bed and began to rub aloe onto his shoulders. Without speaking, Rebecca got out of her bed and started to help him rub it in. Then, she took his hand and led him to her bed. His greasy skin stuck to the sheets. Rebecca turned her back to him and pulled his arm over her, holding tightly onto his hand. His flesh made a wet gurgle as it rubbed against hers. Neither of them said anything for a while. Cliff could smell her suntan lotion. Then Rebecca said, "It's OK."

Cliff whispered, "What are we doing?"

"It's OK."

That summer was when Rebecca started to play with Cliff's testicles. She said it was like rolling dice. That's what she called it, "rolling the dice." Every night that trip she rolled his dice for a long time. She'd go on for ten, fifteen minutes, and then she would take her hand away, pull him close, and say, "It's OK." The years were gone when all she wanted him to do was spin naked in the room so she could watch. Now they saw nothing. He preferred it that way. In the darkness he imagined that she was not his cousin, that what they were doing would last forever. It was the space and time that he felt the most himself. He never wanted the sun to come up. Twice Rebecca rolled over and presented her own back to him and then guided him inside of her. She was already on the pill that summer. It was 1987.

Cliff had promised Rebecca that he would never say anything to anyone about it ever and he hadn't and he never would. He thought about it a lot, though, the fact that they shared this secret. He liked that it was something that Rebecca kept only for him, something she would never share with anyone. And then there was the fact that Cliff had never been with another girl, never really even touched another girl. He had a hard time making friends in general, especially with the opposite sex. Cliff felt strange about how he held on to this secret history, though. It was the history of all that he'd done with his own cousin. Almost every day, in conversation with friends about girls, in watching his classmates, alone in bed, he knew he had both a secret conquest and a bizarre mark. He felt both drawn to the memory and ashamed of it. Still, it offered him a security, a solid item of radioactive potency to which he continually returned. There is always that, he would think. There is always that.

– – –

Rebecca's roommate pushed up the lid of the tanning bed and rose as if from a glowing coffin. A pair of plastic tanning eye-blockers were pulled up on her forehead and her skin shone with sweat.

"You want a beer?" she said.

"OK."

Cliff still couldn't remember her name. Just ask, he thought. He

dice

followed her to a miniature refrigerator in the back of the room. It already felt too late to ask.

"I always thought these mini-fridges were so cute," she said. "I want one."

"Me too," Cliff said. He didn't know what he was talking about, but he just wanted to talk so bad. "Hey, do you want to talk?"

"Sure."

They walked back to the tanning bed and sat with their drinks. The lights were still on and Cliff felt them hot against his bare flesh. It was incredibly bright, and when he looked at the girl she was just a shifting blob against the glow. He tried to relax but was revved up on the stuff. He licked his gums like a wound.

The girl said, "Feel my pulse," and Cliff put his fingers on her wrist. Her blood pumped rapid and insistent below, tapping up at his trembling fingers.

"I feel awesome," she said, then took his hand and placed it above her heart, right on top of her tiny left breast. "Feel it?"

Cliff felt it.

Right then was when the door opened and Rebecca walked in. She still looked so much like Cliff's uncle. She was very thin with bad posture, and her flat blond hair was soaked from the storm. She wore a tight, shimmering dress with a psychedelic kaleidoscope pattern on it, and in the crazy light, Cliff could see that she had waxed off the little moustache she used to have.

For a second Cliff thought that her fiancé wasn't with her, but then a man entered the room. He had two large golden hoop earrings and blond tips in his hair. Several peopled whooped.

"Whoooo!"

"Yeah!"

The man screamed, "Hells yeah!" and ripped off his white shirt. Three white buttons scattered across the linoleum floor. Cliff had never seen anyone rip a piece of clothing off. The first thing he thought was, What is he going to wear home?

As everyone yelled, Cliff looked at Rebecca and she looked directly back at him. He still had his hand on the girl's chest and he felt her heart race even harder as his own did the same. He kept his hand there and started moving it around. He didn't know what he was doing but the girl didn't seem to mind. Rebecca began walking towards them. Cliff nodded at her.

"Well well well!" Rebecca said.

The girl said, "Your cousin's checking my pulse."

This is good, Cliff thought. Check me out, just sitting here naked with this girl, holding her breast. This is me moving on.

Rebecca smiled at Cliff, then looked back at the girl and said, "You know who this is."

"Duh," the girl said.

"He's the one."

"That's what I thought."

Rebecca laughed. "Jesus," she said, sighing. "It is so good to see you, Cliff. Where were you?"

"We were late," Cliff said. He felt like he was floating in some depth of liquid fluorescence. "But what do you mean, 'I'm the one'?"

Rebecca laughed. "I just meant that you're the one. I told her."

"About what?"

Now the other girl laughed, and Cliff felt it jiggle through her miniature breast.

"Cliff. She was my roommate," Rebecca said. She smiled and shook her head, then waved to someone across the room.

Cliff felt like he was starting to panic. The lights were blurring the edges of everything.

"What?" Rebecca said.

dice

"It's just," Cliff said, "I don't know exactly what you're talking about."

"Cliff, please," Rebecca said. "It's no big deal. Cousins do that kind of thing all the time. Like in the old days and stuff."

Cliff felt like every blood vessel in his face was bursting.

"It's OK," the girl said, putting her hand on Cliff's face. "It's OK. Relax."

"No," Cliff said, brushing her hand away. "Wait. I really don't know what you're talking about. What?"

"Cliff. Come on. This isn't a secret anymore," Rebecca said.

The man who had torn his shirt off walked towards them. He had a Celtic design tattooed on his left pec above three Japanese words.

"Hey, come here," Rebecca said. "I want you to meet my cousin. Cliff, this is Stewart. My fiancé."

Stewart said, "What's up, big guy?"

Cliff just looked at him. There were no words, nothing he could say.

"My *cousin*," Rebecca said.

"Wait," Stewart said. "So you're the one . . . that was porking you? Goddamn! No no no. Really, I'm serious. Wait, wait. Really, it's cool. I used to do that all the time. For real, though. Seriously. No, I mean, with my own cousin, Meghan. For real. Wait, man. I know you were just kids. I know you were just kids. Hey. For real. Respect."

Then someone yelled, "Stu-driver!" and Stewart turned.

"Oh shit, Big Dick!" Stewart yelled, then said to Cliff, "One sec," and walked away.

"Relax," the girl said. She put one hand on her chest, on top of Cliff's hand, and reached the other to his eyelids and closed them. Her skin was warm from the tanning bed. "Close your eyes. Yeah.

This is what I do to the kids at daycare, to calm them down. This is what I do before naptime."

Cliff could hear Rebecca, who had walked away and was now talking to Stewart and Big Dick.

Cliff couldn't believe any of this. He felt both righteous and silly, as if his secrets deserved more respect but that it was childish to even care.

The girl continued petting his eyelids.

"Yeah. Relax," she said, then put her other arm around Cliff and lowered him to the surface of the tanning bed. She lay behind him, holding him.

"I . . . uh . . ." Cliff said.

"Shhhh."

It started to work. Cliff began to relax. He saw little red tracers as the girl's fingers passed over his eyelids. It was all so warm. His heart stopped racing and his stomach began to unclench. Cliff could see galaxies. He began to worry that he'd been on the bed too long, that he was burning himself, but then the bed clicked and he heard the electric buzz from all the tanning beds stop. He opened his eyes to darkness. People gasped as they banged into things. Then everyone began talking at once and it became clear that while they'd been inside, Hugo had hit. The hurricane had knocked out the electricity.

The door to the lobby opened and people began finding their clothes and taking them into some sort of light. Cliff realized, stunned, that the sun was already up. Real daylight was shining onto that warm, dark tanning bed. The glow felt judgmental, as if he were standing outside with it, looking in at himself naked with this stranger, all of his secrets laid bare. It felt scary and sobering and urgent. He started to move but the girl held him tighter.

"Shhhh," she said. "Shhhhhh."

dice

She gently pulled his head back down to the tanning bed. The door closed behind the last person and Cliff and the girl were again left in darkness. Cliff could hear the rain now on the roof and wondered if the wedding would be cancelled. The girl put her hand on Cliff's face and closed his eyes again. Her little fingers were still warm and she started up again with the eye petting.

"Shhhh," she said.

She swung a leg over one of his and it felt like his insides were testing all functions at once.

Cliff knew that his parents might wake up and notice that he wasn't in his room at the Red Roof, but he didn't care. This was a chance he might never have again.

In the tiniest whisper, he said, "Will you roll my dice?"

"What?"

He whispered it again, a little bit louder. "Will you roll my dice?"

"I'm sorry. What?"

"Will you roll my dice?"

"I don't think I know what you mean."

Cliff rolled over and looked towards the girl in the dark, where she was lying on the dead fluorescent bulbs. He felt lost in the void, suddenly unsure of how to even speak.

"What is it?" she said. "Just tell me."

His eyelids were tingling. He registered the heat, the sound of continual rain. The absence of electric thrum amplified the weather, huge and encroaching and endless.

"Nothing," he said.

Then a forehead touched his. The other person on that tanning bed was looking right at him. She took his hand and squeezed.

libertee meats

⊝　⊝　⊝　⊝　⊝　⊝　⊝　⊝　⊝

After punching his time card—10:57 PM—Bryce walked upstairs to the locker room. He replaced his Reeboks with a pair of large, sterilized orange rubber boots that rose over his jeans to his knees. He put on a khaki lab coat that hung down to the boots, then pulled on two pairs of gloves: first cotton, then latex over that. Beside the bin of gloves hung a selection of ring knives—short, U-shaped blades protruding from a ring—and he chose one, slowly slipping it over the latex on his right pinky. He then stretched on a hairnet. Bryce was handsome, muscular, and only twenty, but had been going bald since he was sixteen. There was a dark ring of thick hair around his head but only a layer of thin blondish down on the top. Still, they made him wear the hairnet. It was regulation at Libertee Meats.

Leaving the locker room, Bryce could feel the woven plastic settle onto his bald spot. No matter how cold they kept it in there, the hairnet always stuck to a thin layer of moisture on the top of his scalp. Today it was worse than usual. He was still damp from crossing the parking lot in the rain. He hadn't worn a jacket, either, so his T-shirt was soaked to the skin and now, in the air-conditioning, even under the coat, it felt like it was turning to ice.

It had been raining every night for the whole week, but this particular rain was from Hurricane Hugo, which was supposed to be heading straight towards Lystra. On the way to work, WKNC had said Hugo was due to nail Lystra dead on, and Bryce hoped that it would. Huge wind, trees flying, rain in sheets. He was envisioning different storms from movies: *The Final Countdown*, *Back to the Future*, especially *Places in the Heart*. It could be so thrilling.

As his boots squeaked down the stairs, the smell of hotdogs permeated everything—pungent, hickory-flavored meat smell everywhere. The dangling rubber dust guards at the bottom of the staircase led to the main workspace. Here there were no windows, but even without a view, there was one sure sign that it was the middle of the night. During the day, the employees at Libertee Meats were all white, but at night, the shift was almost exclusively Hispanic and black. Of the eleven workers on the graveyard shift, only Bryce and the manager, Gary Malbaff, stood out in their whiteness. It was a hue made even more pronounced by the fact that neither ever saw daylight.

In the center of the room stood the Butcher Boy 8000 grinding and mixing machine. It was stainless steel, about the size of a Winnebago, and it had a little staircase on the side, at the top of which stood Moffett.

Only Moffett worked the mixing machine. He was in his early thirties, one of the two black guys on the graveyard shift, and he had a tattoo of a large crude triangle on his right cheek. His eyesight was terrible and he wore thick, metal-frame glasses. His was the most important job, second to Gary Malbaff's, at Libertee Meats. He controlled the mixing and input of Orange Spice.

Orange Spice was the secret to Libertee Meats. It was a combination of salt and hickory smoke hotdog flavoring, and was called Orange Spice not because it tasted liked oranges, but simply because it was orange. It smelled like hotdog. That smell had nothing to do with cooking. It was all Orange Spice.

The only thing that went into the mixing machine other than Orange Spice was a white, fatty animal byproduct. This was the variety meat: basically the leftovers from a selection of animals that had been processed in every other manner possible. Hearts, brains, feet. As Bryce's dad had always said, "Hotdogs ain't nothing but peckers and lips." And, Bryce thought, he was just about right. He had once seen a cow's eyeball, with eyelashes, in an orange plastic cart of the stuff before it was processed.

▭ ▭ ▭

Bryce had first begun working at Libertee Meats after his wife, Lizz, had given him an ultimatum: he had one week to get a job after he finished his second year at ATCC—Alamance Technical Community College—or else she was going to his mother.

It was clear that Bryce's two years at ATCC weren't going to get him any job in Lystra that he wouldn't have gotten otherwise. He wasn't learning a trade or getting a certificate for anything, he had just been taking classes from the drama pre-major department. He spent all of his time thinking about acting, talking about being an actor. He had never acted in anything, though. He had never auditioned for even as much as a high school play and he was failing almost everything at ATCC.

Lizz herself had never gone to college. She made surprisingly good money, though, waiting tables at Fishbones, a seafood calabash off Highway 70. She killed it with the tips. Still, it wasn't enough. They lived in a crummy neighborhood, so rent was low, but they had a two-year-old son. Heath. He was the reason they had been married so young, and he definitely wasn't cheap. Bryce gave the kid free range. He let him fall and get into things and eat gravel and lick the cat. They were very good friends. Lizz said they had the same mindset.

Bryce could have found a job that at least had normal, daylight hours. He knew this. But during that one-week ultimatum Lizz had given him, after the spring semester had ended and Bryce was supposed to be job hunting, he had instead just smoked pot, watched a *Murder, She Wrote* marathon, and played Nintendo. It was like slowly driving into a wall. He knew what was going to happen but did nothing to avoid it.

So Lizz went to Bryce's mom, who knew Gary Malbaff, and that's how it happened.

All they had open for Bryce at Libertee Meats was a spot on the graveyard shift, 11:00 PM to 7:00 AM. His mom said it would be a good job, that it would be easy. "You know, conveyor belt stuff." She said it was in a cool environment. At first Bryce thought that she was trying to use some hip lingo to convince her kid, but he soon realized that she actually meant cool—that the job was indoors for the summer, that it was well air-conditioned.

◦ ◦ ◦

After Bryce passed through the hanging rubber dust guards, he took one quick glance at the mixing machine. He looked away quickly, though, hoping Moffett hadn't seen, then continued to the Frankomatic with his head down.

Bryce hadn't always been this terrified of Moffett. On his first night, Moffett had shown Bryce how to run the Frankomatic, speaking in a low, husky whisper: "You just do it like this ok cool so you put this here like this see? And then you just want to wait for them to swing by until you cut it right watch this cool ok."

Moffett's Butcher Boy 8000 mixing machine connected to four Vermag Frankomatic sausage handling machines. Each Frankomatic regulated the amount of proto-hotdog mush that got shot into these plastic-type casings, then twisted each dog to separate it from the next. The casings were very thin, and Moffett explained that they would melt away in very high temperatures. Where they melted away to was a total mystery to Bryce, though. As far as he could tell, the stuff just stayed on the dog.

The Frankomatic shot out a constant stream of dogs, which were caught on spinning hooks that hung from a giant, rotating bicycle-type chain. Bryce would let ten to twelve dogs shoot onto the hooks before he would cut the casing with his ring knife and twist the links into a loop. He then lifted the looped dogs with a metal rod and placed them into an orange plastic rolling cart. This was his whole job. Cut the dogs, loop them, lift.

For Bryce's first three weeks, Moffett kept a benevolent eye on him, sometimes bumping fists with him and saying, "What up?" or showing him how to do anything that he couldn't figure out. "You want to save the leftover. See, it gets reused. Put it in here, and then send it back. No, like this." And so on.

One night he approached Bryce with his T-shirt all bunched up around his chest and said, "Hey man, get this zit?"

"What?" Bryce said.

"Get this zit?" he said, motioning towards a raised welt on his back.

"You want me to pop the zit?"

"Yeah. Get it!"

Bryce put his thumbs on either side of the swollen mound and squeezed. A white blob shot out of Moffett's back as if from a miniature tube of toothpaste. Bryce almost gagged.

"Ah. Oh yeah," Moffett said. Then, pulling his shirt back down, said, "Thanks, Brother," and bumped fists with Bryce.

At that moment, Bryce knew he had just done something with Moffett that he would never do with another human, not even his own wife. He looked at his hands, glad to have the latex gloves. This is the graveyard shift in a hotdog factory, he thought.

Moffett's goodwill ended, though, one night in early June. Bryce was cutting a dog with his ring knife, when Moffett walked up and said, "Hey! I saw you looking at me. You looking at me, motherfucker? I see your fucking eyes looking at me. I see your eyes. You want my job? You want to take my job? I will fuck you up!"

Bryce's heart began to pound. He hadn't consciously been

looking at Moffett. He thought about it. Christ. Had he looked over there by accident for a long time? Had he stared at something behind Moffett, something that would have made it look like he was staring at Moffett? No. He hadn't. And how would Moffett even know? He could barely see across the room.

"No," Bryce said. "I don't know what you're talking about. I really . . . I have no idea what you're talking about."

This was just the start. For weeks then, almost every day, Moffett would launch these arbitrary attacks. At some point during this time, Moffett also found out that Bryce had gone to ATCC. This is when Bryce became College Boy.

Bryce couldn't make sense of it. There was nothing. He had done nothing. As far as he could make it, Moffett was just bored and crazy and wanting to fight. Or maybe it was racial. He tried to employ some of the critical cultural analysis that he'd briefly brushed up against in classes at ATCC. Moffett had been working the graveyard shift for three and a half years, but they still hadn't given him a daylight shift. Bryce was the only person on the floor to whom the manager, Malbaff, ever voluntarily spoke. If I worked even remotely as hard as Moffett does, Bryce thought, I bet I'd be working in daylight.

This was uncharted mental territory for Bryce, though. So, after trying to explain to Moffett that he wasn't staring at him, that no he didn't want Moffett's job, that he in fact didn't even plan to work at Libertee Meats for an extended period, that he was hoping to get a job at the Barn Dinner Theater, that yes he was actually hoping to do this (there was always a flyer in the grocery store for auditions— now it was *Guys and Dolls*), after explaining all this, Bryce eventually settled into complete silence.

He spent his silent hours at the Frankomatic thinking about movies, actors, and many actresses. Almost every actress he'd even seen had her own well-thumbed file in his mind, especially Kelly McGillis. He would envision having long conversations with these actresses at dimly lit parties, talking about craft. He would think up specific things that he wanted to say to each actress if he ever met her. He would compliment Debra Winger for her voiceover work in *ET*, maybe ask Sigourney Weaver about working with special effects, and Kelly McGillis—he would ask her if she'd learned to ride a motorcycle just for *Top Gun*, or (as he suspected) was she the type of woman who already knew how.

For a while, Bryce's turn of silence had an effect. Moffett began bumping fists with him again, saying, "What up?" from time to time, or commenting on Malbaff's comb-over. Bryce thought he had passed whatever test he had been put up against.

▱ ▱ ▱

At lunch that night, which came at 1:30 AM, Bryce could hear Hugo on the corrugated metal roof, the rain like gunfire. The radio in the lunchroom was all weather.

Lunch seating was always the same. Bryce ate with the Hispanics and Moffett sat at another table with the one other black guy, Jeff, who worked in the tunnel where the dogs got cooked, where that casing melted away. It was another one of the top-level jobs.

Bryce liked the Hispanic guys. There were seven of them. They either worked the Frankomatics with Bryce or cleaned. The floors in the factory were always covered in animal byproduct and so constantly needed maintenance. This is why everyone wore the giant rubber boots. Jesus Silva, one of the guys who cleaned, didn't speak English at all. He only knew the lyrics to *Paradise City*. Jesus knew Bryce thought it was funny when he sang, and that night at lunch he said, "You take me to Paradise City. The grass is green and pretty!"

Bryce laughed, snorting in bursts, and Moffett turned to him, staring and slowly shaking his head.

These guys at the Hispanic lunch table were always talking about family. About their kids. About girlfriends, ex-girlfriends, ex-wives, girls that had been neither but still had borne their children. Bryce felt included because he could actually join in this conversation. He would talk about his boy, Heath, and joke about Lizz yelling at him for never being around when she was awake. This always got the guys laughing because the ones who spoke English all knew what he was talking about. All of their wives and girlfriends and ex-girlfriends and mothers of their children hated that these men worked the graveyard shift. Bryce hated the shift, too, not only because of Moffett, or the crazy hours, or the fact that he went to sleep at around 9:00 AM after eating dinner and drinking a screwdriver at sunrise, but because he never saw Lizz or Heath. They would be awake when he got home but he was a hotdog-smelling zombie by that point, and when he awoke at sunset, Lizz was at work and Heath was at Bryce's mom's place. Every day he slept in an empty bed.

A few hours after lunch, around 4:30 AM, Bryce was at the Frankomatic, dropping a loop of dogs into the bin and hoping the storm would strengthen, when he noticed that the floor was more slippery than usual. Usually the fatty stuff that splattered onto the floor was slick but contained to single spots. Today, though, the floor was covered in a layer of liquid, much more than usual. He could hear his feet sloshing around in it. Usually he couldn't hear his boots doing anything other than squeak. He dropped the dogs, then shut the Frankomatic off and leaned his pole against the rack with the others. If the machines were leaking at all, even the slightest bit, it meant that all the dogs would be contaminated. Bryce walked up an exposed flight of metal stairs and knocked on the door to Malbaff's office.

"Bryce. Hey there, pal! What can I do you for?" Malbaff said. He set down a huge spreadsheet. His comb-over looked amazing in the fluorescent light—a horrific sculpture of hair.

"I don't know," Bryce said. "Oh, fine, thanks. Look, I don't know, but the floor is really wet."

Malbaff rushed past Bryce to a small metal platform outside the door. From there, it was clear that puddles were forming all over the place.

"Dagblad it!" Malbaff said. "Why didn't somebody get me earlier?" He rushed down the stairs shouting, "Moffett! Moffett!"

Moffett stopped pouring a bag of Orange Spice into the mixer and looked up.

"Turn that thing off. Now!"

Moffett spun to the control panel like it had shocked him and Bryce heard the mixing arm gurgle to a stop. It was never this quiet in the factory. Then Moffett turned and looked through those thick glasses directly at Bryce.

It hadn't taken long for Malbaff to discover that the liquid had been coming not from the mixing machine, but rather from a massive leak in the corrugated metal roof. It was Hugo that had been pouring down the walls and onto the floor, creeping between the machines and puddling up with all that animal waste. There were drains built into the concrete floor, so the actual water hadn't been an issue—it would have been a disaster only if the mixing machine were actually leaking. There was nothing to do other than go back to work.

Just before 6:00 AM, Bryce stood at the Frankomatic with a rod in hand and a loop of links dangling off the end when he heard Moffett say, "Hey, motherfucker!" behind him. He had been waiting for this, trying to prepare mentally. Don't freak out, he told himself. Just ignore him and he'll go away. Just ignore him. But against better logic, he turned. Moffett stood there with his hairnet off. His shaved head glistened. The thick lenses of his eyeglasses caught the fluorescent factory light and glowed. His work coat was too small and fit tightly across his chest. The Frankomatic continued to shoot out dogs beside him, but Bryce didn't move.

"Yeah, bitches," Moffett said. "You want my job? Starting lies about me. Trying to start some shit. You want to start some shit?"

"No, I don't," Bryce said. This was the first time he'd said anything to Moffett for weeks. "And I didn't say anything about you. I just told him that the floor was wet. And also, no. I don't want your job. That's why I'm going to college. Because I don't want your job!"

"You what? Oh shit," Moffett looked around and then started in real quiet, in that scratchy whisper. "I got the shit in my car man a fucking gun in my car after work I am going to fuck you up man I will kill you. You hear me college boy? Bald fucking college boy? Bald fucking gay ass dinner theater college boy?"

Bryce could feel himself shaking. He was actually shaking from fear! He had never consciously noticed himself shaking because of anything other than cold before. He turned his back to Moffett, facing the overload of dogs now dangling from his Frankomatic.

This was when Bryce became aware of himself cinematically, envisioning a camera crew shooting every move. It was the feeling that what he was doing was suddenly worth watching.

"Fuck this!" he said, his voice cracking, and threw the rod onto the ground. It crashed against the poured concrete floor and the dogs bounced into a puddle of water and fat. He pulled his hairnet off and threw it down. Everyone stopped what they were doing and stared. Every small movement felt as if it had a heightened importance, every action choreographed. Bryce was confident that this would be a great film scene. He loved the sensation of being watched. But then the room went dark. The mixing machine gurgled to a stop, and Bryce heard a few dogs fall off his Frankomatic and splash onto the floor. Jesus began to yell in Spanish. Other Spanish answers ensued. Hugo had hit. A red EXIT still glowed dimly in a corner and Bryce began to walk towards it, when he was stopped by a hand on his shoulder.

"That you?" Moffett said. "Hey."

Bryce pulled away.

"I ain't gonna hurt you, man. I can't see shit. Hey!"

Bryce slipped and fell onto his hip, then got up and collided with a rolling cart. He pushed it away and rushed to the door.

Outside, the sun was rising through the chain-link fence, though it was impossible to tell other than the fact that the grey sky was simply becoming a lighter shade of grey in the east. There was no pink glow—it was all extreme rain. It pounded Bryce as he crossed the parking lot at a slow, deliberate pace. He let the water run down his face, from time to time shaking it off or blowing it from his lips. Everyone else was inside, closed in the dark, the Frankomatics just waiting to spring back to life. But even though he was alone in the parking lot, that heightened theatrical rush remained.

Inside his Subaru Brat, as water puddled on the floorboard, Bryce noticed that he was still wearing the orange boots. It didn't matter. They could have his Reeboks. He lit a cigarette and turned the radio on. The coverage was all Hugo. They said that it wasn't clear now if the storm would actually hit Lystra head-on, and this filled Bryce with an improbable rush of disappointment.

The guard waved at Bryce, and it wasn't until Bryce was past the gate that he let it out. Huge, snorting sobs. He was vomiting tears. A bubble of snot emerged from his left nostril and popped. He thought of the scene in *Red Dawn* where Patrick Swayze cried and a snot bubble ballooned from his nose. Just like that, Bryce thought, this performance was real.

Most neighborhoods still had power. Everyone knew what storms did to Lystra, though. Even weak thunderstorms would knock the electricity out. Because of this, Lizz had asked him to buy batteries on his way home. He stopped at the Harris Teeter, a behemoth grocery store that had recently been built. The lot was unusually full for the hour. Inside, people were preparing for disaster, buying tape, batteries, water. A neighbor, Kenny Craven, was buying meat and gave Bryce the head nod. Bryce found a meager selection of double Ds in the home utilities aisle and took an eight-pack before walking to the end, where the aisle emptied out to the meat counter in the back. This was when he saw his wife and child.

Lizz was inspecting a jar of sauerkraut and Heath was in his stroller, buried under a miniature yellow raincoat that Bryce had never seen. Lizz had her back to him, and neither she nor Heath had seen him yet, so Bryce stepped back into the aisle. She'll understand, he told himself. She'll understand. He nodded his head a couple times, pumping himself up, then stepped around a tortilla display. Cutting the corner tight, he walked headfirst into a solid form.

Stepping back, Bryce saw a Harris Teeter employee dressed in white looking down at the floor in befuddlement where a lobster had fallen between his legs. The lobster was alive and still wet, with wide green rubber bands on its claws, claws that were now clicking across the linoleum. In slow-motion panic, an old lady frantically inched out of its path.

"Oh God," Bryce said. "I'm sorry."

He bent down in an effort to reach the lobster, but then realized he was kneeling in the general vicinity of the man's crotch and stood, horrified. He looked at Lizz. She looked back, her face contorted with surprise and concern. Bryce noticed a pack of double D batteries sitting on Heath's lap.

"No," the seafood guy said. "That's OK. That's OK. I'm fine."

"OK. Yeah," Bryce said, aware that Lizz was now wheeling the stroller towards him. "I'm really sorry."

The man started after the lobster.

"What are you doing?" Lizz said.

"I'm buying batteries," Bryce said, holding up the batteries.

"Why aren't you at work?"

"I . . ." Bryce shook his head.

"What?" Lizz said. She sounded scared. "What happened?"

"That guy, Moffett. The one who's always fucking with me?"

"What?" she said again, though clearly she had heard him.

"He thought, I don't know. He just freaked out. He said he was going to shoot me."

"What?"

Bryce watched her freckled brow wrinkle, squeezing her brown eyes into slits.

"So I quit," he said.

"Oh God," Lizz said, then sighed the longest sigh.

"Yeah. I don't know. I can't work there anymore, Lizz. It's horrible. It's been horrible."

"What happened?"

"I told you! This guy said he was going to kill me. I hate it there, Lizz. I hate it. I threw a bunch of hotdogs on the ground," he said, then chuckled. He didn't mean to, but he was trying to grab another emotion—something, anything other than the disappointment he saw settling into Lizz.

"I don't know. I don't know. Yeah, I threw those hotdogs down, and then I left. Ugh," Bryce said. He wasn't getting this across to Lizz at all. "I mean, he told me he was going to shoot me in the parking lot!"

"Who was this? What did you do to him, Bryce?"

"Nothing! That's the whole thing. I didn't do anything to him!"

Bryce thought he'd explained things about Moffett to Lizz before, but then realized that he wasn't sure if they'd ever even spoken about him.

"I hate that job, Lizz. I mean . . . I mean, I never even see you. I can get another job. A real job."

"OK," Lizz said. She kneeled down to comfort Heath, who had started to whimper. "OK."

Then Bryce made an announcement, one he didn't even know was true until he uttered it. "I'm auditioning for the Barn Dinner Theater."

Heath stopped crying and Lizz looked up. She looked exhausted and the last of Bryce's heightened sense of theatricality faded away. This was no movie set. It was surely the Harris Teeter. He became fully aware of his condition, that he was soaking, that he was cold, that he smelled like hotdogs, that he was about to fall asleep, that he was now unemployed and had just knocked a lobster onto the floor.

The people in the aisle had quit staring and the seafood guy was on his knees now, trying to retrieve the lobster from under the tortilla display.

"Bryce," Lizz said.

"Really. I promise this time. I promise. I'm gonna do this myself. I'm going to do it."

But he didn't know what he was going to do. Heath was still whining, and Bryce picked him up, glad to have a distraction.

The next thing that happened was that the electricity in the

friend of the sick

Grier was fifteen and almost naked, standing in her underwear by the blinking light of the digital clock. It pulsed 4:17 AM, flashing red against a thin body just barely female, two mosquito-bite breasts and no curves at all.

"Uncle Pete!" she called. "Uncle Pete!"

She could hear him crying—that was what had just woken her up—but it sounded like he was closed into a thick wall. Grier just stood there, blinking, cocking her ear, until finally she found him. He was outside, on the other side of the window, standing on the air-conditioning unit in the rain.

She slid the window open and rain blew in, cool across her stomach. The neighbors' houses were all dark, suddenly outlined against a diffuse flash of lightning that swelled dull through the low storm clouds.

"C'mere sweetie, c'mere," she said, and Uncle Pete jumped onto the windowsill. Grier burrowed her knuckle into his ear and he started purring strongly, then stepped away for a moment before slashing his claws across her wrist.

"Sugar!" she said, and grabbed the cat by the skin of his neck.

She had seen the vet pick up a cat like this before, but had never done so herself and was somewhat amazed at the maneuver's effect. Uncle Pete dangled limply from her outstretched hand, emitting a low, guttural moan.

What she did next was also something she had never done before. But she was home alone, there was a hurricane blowing into town, and she was scared—of the weather, of the solitude, and now also of the cat. She tossed Uncle Pete back into the rain and slid the window shut.

   □ □ □

Uncle Pete was a white Maine coon cat. When freshly brushed, he took up roughly the same amount of space as a fluffed down pillow. Grier cleaned his litter box, fed him, and let him sleep between her ankles at night, but the cat actually belonged to her best friend and neighbor, Fletcher Hayes.

In May, Fletcher had become sick. It started with a sore in her neck, and then, like lifting an old tire and finding the swarming insect life beneath, they discovered the rest. Lymphoma. Everyone asked Grier about it at school. She gained that strange sudden celebrity, the friend of the sick. Grier promised everyone that Fletcher's chemotherapy was working, but all she really knew was that it had caused Fletcher to start having extreme allergic reactions to Uncle Pete. When she'd hold him, red blotches would immediately begin to rise on her face. Her nose would run. She'd start to wheeze and itch. Fletcher wouldn't get rid of Uncle Pete, though. She adored him. So Grier had taken him in until Fletcher was well again.

   □ □ □

Grier couldn't fall back asleep. The house was too silent, too empty. She was too keenly aware of being inside it alone. Her mother had gone to the coast that afternoon, *towards* the storm that was due to hit tonight, driving to Wilmington with Fletcher's parents so they could board up the condo they co-owned. They'd left Fletcher in the care of her older brother Mike next door.

As the storm picked up, Grier lay awake, concerned about Uncle

friend of the sick

Pete. He was Fletcher's constant object of affection. Even though he made her sick, Fletcher still insisted on seeing Uncle Pete at least daily for the kitty kiss. The kitty kiss was what Fletcher called it when she would blow softly at Uncle Pete, who would then lift his nose to her mouth, intently sniffing for as long as Fletcher could exhale, his nose bouncing lightly against her puckered lips.

Grier had almost decided she needed to go find him, to bring him back inside, when a soft knocking came from the window. She wrapped the bedsheet around her shoulders and slowly crossed the room. This time, it wasn't Uncle Pete. It was Fletcher's brother Mike. He was eighteen, and wore a black trench coat, and his hair, usually a rigid six-inch red mohawk, now hung limp and wet across his scalp. Grier's heart raced as she opened the window.

"You up?" Mike said.

"Sort of."

"I saw your light on."

"Uncle Pete freaked out. Look."

Grier's wrist had three large gashes across it. They were still bleeding. Mike gently held her arm, turning it in the light.

"Where is he?" Mike said.

"Outside."

"Outside?"

In the road, a streetlamp lit the rain falling diagonally, tree limbs bent and swaying.

"I tried to get him in through the window," she said. "But he was freaking out."

Mike kept looking outside.

"We have to go get him," he said.

"I know."

- - -

Two days after her first round of chemo, Fletcher admitted to Grier in tears that her pubic hair had collected in her underwear and fallen out upon the bathroom floor. That night Grier slept over. Fletcher fell asleep early and Grier stayed up with Mike, running lines from *Guys and Dolls*, the play they were both performing with the Barn Dinner Theater.

The main reason Grier had even auditioned was that she knew Mike would be in it. He acted in everything the Theater did. Grier had never acted in anything before, but she had had a crush on Mike since she was five years old and thought this was finally her chance to spend time with him. Fletcher had an uncontrollable jealousy about any of her friends interacting with Mike—less an attachment to Mike than to her friends, it seemed. He was a freak. A theater nerd with a mohawk. Fletcher did everything she could to distance herself from him. Once, during a party, she found Mike making out with one of her swim team teammates—short, blond, cute Ashley Aikens—and proceeded to tip the gasoline out of the neighbor's lawn mower and onto Mike's skateboard, then light it on fire in the front yard.

That night in the kitchen, with Fletcher asleep down the hall, neither of them could remember their lines. After a while Mike said, "You want to just role-play?"

"OK," Grier said.

Mike then closed his eyes and wiped a hand slowly down his face. This was a technique their director, Ms. Astor, had taught them to cleanse themselves of the real world, to enter the realm of acting. Once Mike was clean, he said, "I'm gonna show you what they do at the doctor. It's like this. They go, 'I'm going to have to inspect your glands. Turn your head to the side.'"

He inspected Grier's neck.

"How does it look?" she said.

"Bad. Real bad. Let me see your retina."

She turned and Mike brought his face so close to hers that she could feel his breath. She wondered if this was what the kitty kiss was like, if this was the way Uncle Pete felt when Fletcher put her face near his, because if so, then it all made sense to Grier, because she wanted Mike to stay there, breathing on her face forever.

Grier stayed in the guest room that night because she was afraid of waking Fletcher. At some point after Grier had fallen asleep, Mike came into the room. She woke up when he climbed onto the mattress. Neither spoke as he put his arms around her. They just clung to each other as if, if either let go, the other might fall off the bed.

○ ○ ○

Outside, Grier's terrycloth robe quickly grew heavy with the rain. Inland North Carolina always got weather like this, unraveling hurricanes dropping huge amounts of rain as they blew in across the Piedmont. Grier and Mike crossed into Mankin Park, the open plot across the street from their houses, where a small creek ran. The water was just starting to overflow the creek's banks, rising up a small bridge that had red lines painted onto one of its supports, marking the floodcrests of years past. Five feet in 1973, six and a half in '82. There were more, some washing off, dozens up and down the concrete. Above '82 someone had painted WHIRLIES.

They walked the park for several minutes, looking up into the swaying dark branches, rain dripping into their eyes, slipping on wet grass, kneeling and calling Uncle Pete's name into bushes, before finally coming to a stop on the bridge.

"This is pointless," Mike said, and wrapped his warm hand around Grier's. It was thrilling, this casual affection unhidden. She imagined them holding hands at school, at the mall. On the front steps. It could never happen, though. Not if there was a chance Fletcher would find out. She let herself imagine, just for a moment, what a world without Fletcher would be like, what new freedoms she would have. She held on to Mike and looked at the water rising dark and glimmering below. She had an urge to dive in and swim through what was usually air. She felt invincible. She smiled at Mike beside her and he wiped his hand down his face. Then he held his hand before his mouth as if he were holding a microphone and said, "I am Walter Teague with your First Alert Forecast! And I'm here live in Mankin Park tonight as Hurricane Hugo moves into Lystra. Here's a local woman. Ma'am, were you prepared for this storm?"

He held the invisible microphone to Grier.

Grier froze. Mike's hand was so close to her face, almost touching her nose. She could see dirt under his thumbnail, could smell the mud on his hand. She could think of nothing to say. She just stood there and smelled his fingers. This was when she saw the young woman standing on the end of the bridge under the streetlamp like a ghost in a large wool hat, holding an umbrella that glowed red against the darkness. It was Fletcher. She looked around, seeming removed and confused.

"Uncle Pete came to my window," Grier said.

"You shouldn't be out in this," Mike said.

"It's Uncle Pete shouldn't be out in this," Fletcher said.

"We'll find him."

She kept looking around, squinting into the darkness, before finally just looking at Grier.

"What are you guys doing?"

"We're looking for Uncle Pete," Grier said.

"He can't be out in this," Fletcher said. "He really just . . . he can't . . ."

She then moved slowly back into the darkness, almost sleep-walking. Moments later, a thin sliver of light appeared in her front doorway across the lawn, profiling her body as it slid back inside.

"Motherfucker," Mike said.

"I have to go talk to her," Grier said.

"No you don't."

"Yes I do," Grier said, and rushed across the road, through the soggy lawn to Fletcher's back door. She stepped into the kitchen, where the refrigerator held a magnetically arranged display of get-well cards. Every second grader at Preston Elementary had made one for Fletcher after the student body president at their high school organized the effort. It was a surprise and he delivered the box of cards one afternoon accompanied by a few of the children. Grier had been with her when they arrived, and Fletcher had been mortified. Beside that refrigerator was the table where Grier had first role-played with Mike. Fletcher's house was filled with memories like this. There was the stereo that, a few summers earlier, Grier and Fletcher had used to continually play a cassette of the rap group Whodini. They had memorized the lyrics and choreographed dances, and then, in September of that year, when Grier's parents had divorced and her father had left, Fletcher had sat Grier down at that table, pressed play on the box, and rapped along to the Whodini song "Friends." Afterwards, she said, "See. That's what we are. *Friends.*"

She walked down the hallway, past the guest room where Mike had held her, past the bathroom where Fletcher's pubic hair had spilled out upon the floor, and stopped in the doorway of Fletcher's bedroom.

Fletcher lay on her mattress. Her scalp was smooth and soft, as if a thin layer of uncooked dough had been spread across it.

"Hey," Grier said.

"Did you find him?"

"Not yet," Grier said. Fletcher rolled over and looked silently at the ceiling. "Fletcher?"

"I just don't feel very good." Grier stepped closer. Fletcher looked tired, old, and shrunken. She shut her eyes and said, "Can you get Mike?"

Grier found Mike in the kitchen. By the time they returned to her bedroom, Grier was positive Fletcher was dead. It makes perfect sense, she thought. This is what cancer does.

But then Mike said, "When she's out like this, she doesn't get up for, like, ever. It's because of the drugs and stuff. She takes all these drugs."

He spoke at full volume and Fletcher didn't stir. Then he took Grier's hand again and led her to his bedroom. Only as a girl had she been in Mike's room before, marveling at his mess, looking at his official boy items—his skateboard, his soccer ball when he had been younger, his sneakers, his tapes. He put his arms around her and she nestled her face into his neck, smelling the cherry Jell-O in his hair. Every morning he heated a small bowl of it in the microwave, then rubbed the liquefied gelatin into his hair to keep the mohawk standing. Grier thought it smelled great. Mike pushed her head back and started to kiss her. She kissed back and they fell onto the bed.

"It's OK," he said. "She's not going to wake up."

Grier sat on top of him, straddling him, and he grinned up at her through the darkness. She felt suddenly rash and safe, and wiped a hand down Mike's face, from forehead to chin, then did the same to herself. They were clean, ready for escape.

"It's nice to meet you, Walter Teague," she said.

"Who are you?"

"Local woman."

"What do you do?"

"I'm a doctor."

"What kind?"

"A heart doctor."

"How is it?"

Grier put her head against his damp chest. "It's beating."

"Do I sound healthy?"

"I don't know."

It seemed contact was some necessary medicine. They grabbed at each other desperately, licking each other's mouths and faces. Her wet robe fell to the floor with a *splat*. He took his clothes off in only a few rapid motions. They touched each other everywhere. Grier lay with one leg swung over Mike's, listening to his slow, deep breathing. It was the longest she had ever spent touching a boy's body. The wind buzzing through the low pine branches outside was loud enough that she did not hear Fletcher step into the doorway, only saw her head when it appeared, alien and thin against the dim hall light.

"Mike," Fletcher said. "I'm sick."

Mike flinched and turned on the bedside lamp. Grier clenched her eyes against the sudden light, but when she opened them again, it seemed Fletcher hadn't even noticed that she was there. She was simply leaning against the doorframe, covering her face with her hands. A thin strand of saliva dangled from between her wrists.

Mike turned the light off as he rushed into the bathroom. Grier lay silently in the darkness.

"Can you just get me a glass of water?" Fletcher finally said, so faintly that there was no way Mike could have heard.

Grier said nothing.

"I'm just so thirsty," Fletcher whispered. "Please, Grier."

"Oh! OK, yeah."

She pulled on Mike's T-shirt and rushed to the kitchen, passing Fletcher on the way, rubbing against her in the doorway. When she returned, Fletcher was sitting on the floor, her back against the doorjamb. Pepto-Bismol was spilled across her T-shirt. It was such a bright pink. It seemed the color of sickness.

"If I die, you guys will have each other," Fletcher said.

"What are you talking about?" Mike said.

"I'm talking about this."

"Stop saying that."

Then she burped up the rest of her Pepto-Bismol and it ran pink down her chin and onto her ankles. Mike helped her down the hall to her room.

Grier sat on the edge of Mike's bed, waiting, looking at his posters. The Violent Femmes. Christian Hosoi. The Connells. Lance Mountain. She stepped into the hallway and listened but heard nothing. She didn't know if she should stay or go. After several minutes, she put on her wet robe and walked outside.

It was just barely daylight and the area of yard between the two houses was littered with small branches. The rain was even stronger, more steady, and the wind was beginning to gust. There were no insects, usually a chorus at this hour. It was all just continual rain, thudding into the grass and washing through the leaves. In the park the water had risen over the first floodmarker on the bridge and now lapped the concrete just below '82.

The lights in Fletcher's bedroom cast a pale parallelogram onto the grass outside, and Grier could see Mike standing in the room near the glass. She thought that he was waving and she waved back, but then realized he was only unfolding a large towel, and for a moment she let her hand dangle in midair, as if something delicate, like a brittle marionette, were hanging from her fingertips.

This was when the lights shut off in Fletcher's bedroom. Grier looked around. The streetlamp was out, the light over her back door was dark. The whirring of the air-conditioning unit ground to a halt. It wasn't uncommon for the electricity to fail in Lystra, the result of too many old trees and thunderstorms, but it startled her and she rushed back to her own house.

Inside, she took off her cold robe and showered in the dark bathroom in an attempt to warm herself up. The shower seemed almost exotic in the darkness and she tried to relax. She inhaled deep lungfuls of steam. Afterwards, as she dressed, she looked outside as a trash can rolled onto the lawn and what seemed to be a candle floated through the darkness in Mike's kitchen.

In the back hallway, the door was banging in the wind. Its top hinge was broken. At one point Grier's father had fixed it with a broken nail, but now it had broken completely and often kept the door from closing all the way. She started towards it, then heard Uncle Pete meow. She found him at her feet, soaked, looking half his size. She bent down and he strained his neck towards her, trying to reach her face. It was clear what he wanted: the kitty kiss. She picked him up instead, his claws digging into her flesh. He cried and tried to pull away, but she held him tightly and rushed into the rain.

The trash can rolled away from her on a new gust of wind, a plastic bag lifting out of it on the draft, floating in a spiral into the low branch of a dogwood. The water in the park had obliterated any suggestion of the actual creek from which it came and now spread thin across the grass, lapping at iron bench legs and tree trunks and inching even closer to WHIRLIES on the bridge.

She approached Mike's back door and through the small window saw the candle now burning on the kitchen table. When she swung the door open, though, she found Fletcher, not Mike. A mug of something steaming sat on the table before her and she looked like a zombie, her eyes sunken in, the skin puffy and dark around them.

Grier didn't say anything, just set Uncle Pete on the kitchen table. As Uncle Pete rushed across it, Fletcher pursed her lips and closed her eyes. When he reached her, they began the kitty kiss. Uncle Pete stood frozen except for his tail, which continued to whip back and forth. Grier watched, unbelieving, as it passed in and out of the small candle flame. It seemed too impossible, too ridiculous to be true as the very tip suddenly blossomed into flame. Fletcher's eyes were still closed, though, and Uncle Pete seemed oblivious, his purring audible even from a few feet away. The flame burnt brightly for an instant but then, upon encountering the dense wet fur a bit farther up, faded and died. The whole event lasted no more than three seconds.

In the dim candlelight, hives were already appearing on Fletcher's scalp like mysterious continents revealing themselves on a map. A small bulb of mucus emerged from a nostril and began to creep down her upper lip. But still she continued to exhale. When Fletcher finally took in a new breath, Grier knew she was going to smell the thick, foul stench of burnt cat hair. But for now, Fletcher looked elated, high, and not even Uncle Pete had noticed himself on fire, too intent on getting some good love from whoever would give it.

quickening

∘ ⸺ ∘ ⸺ ∘ ⸺ ∘ ⸺ ∘ ⸺ ∘ ⸺ ∘ ⸺ ∘ ⸺ ∘

       Isaac turned the school bus left at Church's Chicken, past the abandoned strip mall on the right with the two dead cars parked in it. Kudzu twisted up the antenna of one.

"Nimbostratocumulus?" he said.

"Nope," Scoville said. Scoville was eight years old, black, had a bumpy shaved head, and talked big. "There ain't no nimbostrato. It's just nimbo. Or strato."

"Well, which one is it?"

In the rearview mirror, Isaac watched Scoville consult his study sheet.

"This one's strato."

"Strato, nimbo," Isaac said, now barreling through a wide expanse of standing water. Past the parking lot, he spotted the Mylar balloon that had been tangled in the power lines for days, all of its helium almost gone now as it whipped back and forth in the wind. This was the route he drove daily, from 6:00 to 8:00 AM and 2:00 to 4:00 PM. He was driving an early return trip now, though, because the hurricane had cancelled school and he hadn't even heard until it was too late. Neither had Tisha and Scoville, the two third graders now on the bus—two of the only four students who'd shown up that morning. He should have put it together. It wasn't until he had driven them all the way to school that they found out it was closed and Isaac's father, the bus dispatcher, had sent them back. Now Isaac was driving Scoville and Tisha home.

"What's the nimbo?" he said.

"Nimbo are the cotton ball–looking ones."

"They all look like cotton balls."

He came to a halt at their bus stop—a postal box on a corner without curbs or a sidewalk, only a drainage ditch now overflowing.

"OK, Strato," Isaac said. "Which house is yours?"

"It's further down," Scoville said.

"That one's mine," Tisha said.

Tisha was also in Scoville's class but she already towered above him, lanky and rail thin and awkward in her movements, like a newly born horse. Her jeans all had elastic waists and her eyes bugged out over a long crooked nose. She was pointing through the steamy windows at a large, dilapidated house with intricate, rotting trim. Antennas sprouted from dormers and a nest of mailboxes hung clustered by the door. This part of town was filled with once grand houses like this, now run-down and segmented. The black part of Lystra. Brown Town, Isaac's friends called it. The Place Where People Are Shot.

Isaac liked driving this route, though. He felt he was keeping things real, getting closer to the source, because in reality, he wasn't just a school bus driver. He was a singer. He specialized in obscure spirituals that he learned from archival recordings at the public library. He was not a believer, but the authenticity of these songs appealed to him. Songs with names like "Hang Man Johnny" and "Wrestling Jacob," "Lilies Walk Out of the Valley" and "Oh Oh Oh Jesus!" By his senior year in high school, Isaac had already begun booking shows in the area. He sang in public libraries and rock clubs, selling tapes of himself out of a suitcase after shows. A few times he had even sung in some of the area's black churches, bringing the lost spirituals back to the source.

Tisha's house was dark, foreboding.

"Anyone home?" Isaac said.

"I don't know."

quickening

Isaac considered all that could go wrong with a child alone in a storm. Downed power lines started fires. Gas lines broke. Limbs fell though roofs. He couldn't just leave her.

"We're all going in."

Inside, the electricity was out but the dim natural light created a series of geometric shadows across a once elegant flight of wooden stairs, at the top of which Tisha unlocked a green door with the muted topography of countless layers of paint. Weak sunlight shone through the apartment onto brushed-aluminum chairs beside a chrome and glass dining table. The room looked antiseptic and polished. Isaac was surprised at the modern aesthetic.

"Mom?" Tisha called.

There was no answer.

"Where's your house?" Isaac asked Scoville.

"Down there."

Through the window, Isaac saw two young black men in enormous sweatshirts sharing a cigarette under the eave of a pink house.

"We're going to wait here," he said.

"Why?" Scoville said.

"It's not safe."

"That's just Jorge and Jorge."

"I mean the weather."

"Why you keep looking at your watch?" Scoville said.

"I have a doctor's appointment."

"You sick?"

"No, it's my girlfriend."

"She sick?"

"No. Let's get you into something dry. There anything here, Tisha, any dry clothes that Scoville might borrow?"

"Maybe."

Tisha led Scoville through a door near the kitchen and Isaac checked his watch again.

His girlfriend, Emily, was five and a half months pregnant. Recently she had had what the doctor called the quickening—the first time a mother feels the child move in the womb. Since those first subtle quivers, though, the child had become hyperactive, kicking and turning as Emily's pale stomach rose visibly. The only thing they found that would calm it down was music. Emily had begun placing headphones on her belly and playing Beethoven into the flesh. She said it would raise the child's IQ. Isaac didn't know about that, but he did know that if they put those headphones on when the child began one of its episodes, the movement invariably ceased. Isaac found it to be profound. He felt like there needed to be some sort of scientific study done on their baby. Clearly the child was listening.

Emily had an appointment in eleven minutes. Waiting for Scoville to change, Isaac knew he wasn't going to make it. He liked to go to all of her doctor's appointments. They made him feel more in control of his destiny, a confidence rapidly decreasing. He was only twenty. He wasn't ready for a baby.

Through the windows, Isaac could now see the cumulonimbus clouds low in the sky and knew what was happening above. Spinning nimbostratus, arcs of hovering water, shifting and condensing and now falling onto Lystra. Since Hurricane Hugo had been on the news, the children had been studying the weather for the past week, learning storm patterns and clouds. Cumulus. Altocumulus. Stratocumulus. He was amazed at the number of names for the same natural phenomenon. Clouds. That's all he had thought of them as before. Isaac often helped the children study on the bus. He found that most of the materials—like the presidents, the state capitals, the Pledge of Allegiance—were things he felt he should know but did not.

"You guys OK?" he said, tapping on the door. There was a rush of movement from within. He wasn't sure how long this should take. Something seemed strange, though. He swung the door open.

Inside, Scoville stood completely naked near the foot of a bed, his small buttocks a slighter shade of pink against his dark back. Tisha was in her underwear, sitting Indian style on the mattress with clothes piled around her.

"Whoa!" Isaac said.

"Give it to me," Scoville said, and Tisha held a yellow dress to him.

"What's going on?"

"She made me show her my privates."

"They're my clothes," Tisha said, stepping into a pair of pink overalls.

"Tisha!" Isaac said. "You do not make other people do that!"

Scoville was pulling the dress over his head.

"Tisha. Jesus," Isaac said. He had no idea how to handle this. The yellow dress fell over Scoville's head and pooled around his feet. "Look, is there anything else he could wear?"

"No."

"He could fit into your jeans."

"Those all I got," she said, pointing towards the ones she had just removed, now seeping water into a dark outline on the hardwood floor.

"OK, guys," Isaac said. "OK. Look. Scoville. Let's pretend we're playing dress-up. That's all it is. OK?"

"I don't mind," Scoville said.

"We playing dress-up?" Tisha said.

"No. I'm just saying that it's like Scoville's wearing a costume. Think of it like that. A dry costume."

"You said we were playing dress-up," Tisha said.

"We're not gonna play?" Scoville said.

"I didn't say that. We'll play something, if you want."

Isaac desperately tried to think of a game to play with the children. He wondered if they were too old for hide-and-seek.

"Bag-heads?" Tisha said.

"Bag-heads!" Scoville said.

"OK," Isaac said. He didn't know what they were talking about.

Tisha rushed into the kitchen and Scoville followed, dragging the yellow skirt across the floor behind him. From between the refrigerator and the counter, Tisha retrieved three Kroger paper bags and laid them on the floor.

"We make them like this in class," she said, drawing a green crayon mouth onto a bag. Then she rapidly drew five eyes, all with very long black eyelashes, and punched small holes through two. She put it over her head.

"Wow," Isaac said.

Scoville drew what amounted to a pumpkin face on his bag—two triangle eyes above a toothy grin. He put it on and looked back and forth between Tisha and Isaac.

Isaac wasn't sure if he should play this game or just supervise. The kids were now looking closely at him. Or he assumed they were. He couldn't see either of their faces, but both bag-heads were pointed in his direction. He drew a woman's face onto his bag, adding large red lips and long curling lashes. When he put it over his head, the children burst into laughter.

"You like this, huh?" he said.

The laughter increased.

"Do I look like your mother?" he said, now speaking in a high falsetto.

"No!" Tisha screamed, laughing.

"Are we sisters?"

"No!" Scoville said.

"I think we look like sisters."

The children squealed from behind their paper masks. Isaac thought he must remember to play bag-heads with his own child when the time came. Knowing about something like this, he thought, this is what makes the difference. These are the things that parents do. He felt suddenly empowered, and then began to sing.

"Um diddle diddle diddle um diddle ay! Um diddle diddle diddle um diddle ay! Supercalifragilisticexpialidocious!"

▱ ▱ ▱

As a boy, Isaac had listened to his mother's *Mary Poppins* record endlessly, and those songs were some of the first he had ever learned. She had sung them to him during afternoons in the yard, or hiding together under tablecloth tents. When Isaac was seven, though, his mother had died from spinal meningitis. Isaac had not been raised in the denomination, but his mother's family were the only Russian Orthodox in Lystra and the funeral had included a traditional open casket. The body looked almost exactly like his mother alive, asleep. The coloring was perfect, and the distance Isaac kept from it allowed the illusion to live. Isaac now felt that it was important to see the body at a funeral, to allow the mourners to experience the physical closure of a coffin snapping shut, but at that time, when the priest let the lid fall, it had been violently painful to Isaac, like a hand smothering his face. What helped him past it, though, in that initial moment, was the fact that he was expected to sing. In retrospect, it seemed a job perhaps too great for a seven-year-old, but something about the responsibility of a public task forced Isaac to cast off that unbearable burden. He stood at the altar and sang the hymn "The Day Thou Gavest, Lord, Is Ended," and it gave him a moment of peace. He still believed greatly in that power, the escapist power of music.

— — —

"The biggest word I ever heard, and this is how it goes—oh! Super-califragilisticexpialidocious!"

Before the next line, Isaac heard the door open. He turned in its direction, but could not locate it through the eye holes.

"What the hell?" a woman said.

Isaac ripped off the bag-head.

A thin black woman in a nurse's uniform stood inside the door. She looked to be about the same age as Isaac.

"Baby!" the woman said.

"I know this looks crazy," Isaac said.

"You get the hell away from her," the woman said, rushing to Tisha.

"I'm her bus driver."

The woman began backing Tisha into a corner.

"No you aren't."

"No, I am. School is closed. I'm her bus driver."

"He is, Mom," Tisha said.

"Ma'am," Isaac said. "I am telling you the God honest truth. I am her school bus driver and was just playing with your daughter here until you came home. I didn't get the news that school had closed."

"Baby," Tisha's mother said, petting Tisha's hair back from where the bag had made it stand up on the side. "Baby." Then she looked at Scoville, who still wore his bag-head and was looking at them through its triangle eyes. "Who's she?"

Scoville took the bag off and Tisha's mother said, "Jesus."

"Hey, Miss Reynolds," Scoville said.

"What's that dress for, baby?"

"My clothes're wet."

"Oh Lord," she said, then looked at Isaac and squinted. "How I know you?"

"I drive her bus."

"No. I know you. You sang at Mount Hope Church."

Isaac had sung at an Easter celebration there in April.

"Yeah, OK," Isaac said.

"What'd you sing?" Tisha said.

"He sang some songs, some different songs," her mother said.

"Where was I?" Tisha said.

"Different?" Isaac said.

"You were with your daddy."

"What'd you sing?" Tisha said.

"Some old songs," Isaac said. "Real old."

"Those were old songs?" her mother said.

"That's right."

"Alright. And you drive buses, too?"

"Yeah."

"Well, you can see why I thought you were trouble."

"Yes ma'am."

"So. You gonna need me to watch him?" she said, nodding towards Scoville.

"I can't leave him with anyone other than his parents," Isaac said.

"What you going to do with him?"

"Take him with me. Scoville?"

Scoville shrugged and folded his bag-head in half.

The rain had picked up, the streets were filling with branches, and the traffic lights were out, so Isaac drove slowly as Scoville inspected his folded yellow sheet of notebook paper. He had taken off the yellow dress and changed back into his wet clothes.

"Gimme one," Isaac said.

"Cirrostratus."

"OK. Those are the high ones? The ones that are mostly just ice?"

"Yeah. Tisha's mom almost just whup you, didn't she?"

Isaac just continued to drive. After a few moments, a siren sounded in the distance, growing louder.

"Doppler effect," Scoville said. "How they use that to tell weather?"

They had studied this phenomenon in part of their forecasting segment, how sound waves change shape when coming from a source that is either approaching or departing. For days the children had been talking about it after the local weatherman, Walter Teague, had visited the school. Isaac had no idea how they used it to forecast weather, though.

"They must bounce sound waves off clouds or something," he said. "Track it like radar."

"Oh yeah. That's right," Scoville said. "That's exactly what it is."

The siren faded, its pitch dropping as they rumbled through huge puddles. The bus seemed louder without a full load of passengers, loose windows and bolts announcing themselves in a constant rattling clamor.

"What's wrong with your girlfriend?" Scoville said.

"Nothing."

"Why's she going to the doctor?"

"She already went."

"Why?"

"She's pregnant."

"How many kids you have?"

"None yet."

"You old, though."

At Preston Elementary, the rolling door to the garage was pushed up, and in the overhang of the opening Isaac's father sat in a lawn chair beside Emily. Even from the bus, Isaac could see her abdomen rising in her lap. The other morning, she had told Isaac of a dream she had had that she was full term, nearing labor, but that her stomach had not grown at all. Instead, the baby was just clearly outlined under her taut flesh, as if it had been shrink-wrapped in skin.

He parked the car and rushed Scoville through the rain.

"I am so sorry," he said, wiping rain off his face under the shelter of the overhanging garage door. "Their parents weren't home so I waited I didn't know what to do I just— One of their moms came home but his parents weren't home yet so I figured we'd just wait here. I left a note. What'd they say?"

"They didn't say anything," Emily said.

"They just said it was normal?"

"They did an ultrasound and she was fine."

"You saw her?"

Emily smiled.

"She look like?"

Emily shrugged. "It's hard to describe. Nothing, sort of. She was moving, but not like what she'd been doing."

"I wanted to be there," Isaac said. "You think I was dead or something?"

"Just figured you were driving."

Emily was never as worried about anything as he was.

"This is Scoville."

"Hi, sweetie."

"Hey, Son," Isaac's father said. "Relax."

Isaac unfolded a lawn chair beside Emily, then slumped into it and sighed as Scoville sat on a bench against the inside wall and continued to study his clouds. Isaac gently squeezed Emily's shoulder, feeling the bone shallow under the skin.

The three of them were silent for a moment, watching the rain push through the gravel. A thin branch on a scrub pine at the edge of the lot twirled in the wind, hanging by one thin, resilient wooden sinew.

"What'd you do with them?" Emily said.

"With who?"

"The kids."

Isaac looked at Scoville. He was engrossed in the clouds, mouthing the names silently to himself with his eyes closed.

"Nothing," Isaac said. "We just waited."

After a while, Scoville perked up when the forecast came on the battery-powered radio. As they listened, the headlights of a white pickup truck flashed towards them.

"That's my mom," Scoville said.

The car stopped close alongside the garage and the window rolled down. A young black woman with a red baseball hat said, "Get."

Scoville ran to the passenger side and climbed in. The woman then stepped out of the truck. She was round and very dark skinned, wearing a blue plastic raincoat with large yellow daisies printed on it. She stood in the rain, the windshield wipers of the truck flinging water behind her.

"You the bus driver?" she said.

"Yeah."

"Elizabeth Reynolds said she come home and find you in her place with a bag on your head and my boy in a dress."

"You're gonna have to get back in your car, ma'am," Isaac's father said.

"Dad," Isaac said. "Hold it a second. I know it sounds crazy, ma'am, but we were just playing."

"Am I crazy?" the woman said. "Because if I am, then tell me. But it sounds like something messed up was going on in that girl's home. My boy in a bag and a dress." She looked at Emily. "You his wife?"

"I'm his girlfriend."

"Mmm, mmm, mmm," she said, shaking her head and looking at Emily's stomach.

"OK. Right now," Isaac's father said, standing up.

"Dad."

Isaac's father began walking towards her, slowly emerging from the garage into the rain.

"I'm going to call the police," he said.

"I'm gonna call the motherfucking police," Scoville's mother said.

"My son loves you people and you shit on him. *Shit* on him."

"Dad."

"You people?"

"Dad! Jesus Christ."

Scoville's face hovered behind the clouded windshield. Isaac felt like something was about to explode.

"Jim," Emily said. "Hey, Jim."

Isaac had never heard Emily use his father's first name before. He had never heard anybody his age use his father's first name. His father stopped walking but continued to stand there in the rain, guarding the entrance of that garage like a bear before his den.

Scoville's mother finally got back into her truck, and it wasn't until after she left that Isaac noticed Emily holding her belly. Over the phone, the doctor had assured her that the fits didn't mean anything was wrong, that they were fairly common and might even be a good sign, but right now she looked scared and in pain and betrayed by her own body.

"Is she freaking out?" Isaac said.

"Yeah."

"OK. She's freaking out."

He touched the taut skin across Emily's abdomen and it felt like a cat caught inside of a bag: little angles—tiny elbows and knees, he guessed, barely human, maybe see-through, he didn't know—kept pushing out. His father knelt beside him and put his own hands on Emily's stomach. Emily held herself, too. There were six hands now—the whole family holding her writhing flesh.

"It's cool," Isaac said. "It's cool."

Emily took a deep breath, but the movements weren't slowing.

Isaac put his chin on her stomach and started to sing. "There Is a Balm in Gilead" was the first thing that came to mind, and he sung directly into the flesh. After two verses, it didn't seem to be working. He switched to "We Are Climbing Jacob's Ladder," but it, too, made no difference and he stopped, looking at his knuckles as Emily's deep breathing and the radio filled the silence. The weatherman still listed windspeeds and rainfall amounts as gusts of spray blew into the garage. The three of them sat in silence for several moments, Isaac unsure of what to say. He was scared of the pain of another, afraid of what this meant about how he would react during actual labor.

Then Emily said, "You really do that?"

"What?"

"Really play with the kids?"

"Yeah," Isaac said. "I played with them."

Emily kept her eyes closed, head thrown back, and a small smile spread across her face. Unseen limbs continued to lift the flesh on her stomach.

Isaac's father picked up the radio and said, "Try this."

"For what?"

He pushed it against Emily's flesh. The forecast was suddenly muted, the weatherman's voice now distant and low.

"Find some music," he said.

Isaac began looking for the knob, but before he could change the channel, the weatherman began listing all the counties under

quickening

flood alert—*"Carteret, Pamlico, Craven, Lenoir"*—and as he did, less elbows, fewer see-through knees, seemed to strike Isaac's palm.

"Cumberland, Wake, Chatham, Montgomery . . ."

Isaac hadn't been positive at first, but the movement was clearly slowing now.

"Pender, Bladen, Cabarrus . . ."

Isaac looked up. Emily's head was thrown back, the roof of her mouth briefly glistening as she took a deep breath. *"Mecklenburg, Guilford . . ."* the list just wouldn't stop. There were so many counties Isaac had never heard of. He wondered if they might study them on the bus one day.

"Yadkin, Catawba, Alleghany . . ."

The music of these counties strung on, intoned through transistor to flesh, and Emily's abdomen finally became calm. Isaac waited for another kick but there was nothing. Beneath his damp palms, encased in flesh and bone, Emily's hidden passenger had been mesmerized by the various names of this wide flooding state.

MORNING

The storm continues to chug to the northwest at this hour, the eye now becoming less defined as it crosses over Yadkin County to the south of us. So the rain, heavy rain, continuing yet, but the storm path is tracking further westward. For us in the Piedmont? That means we're going to miss this guy. Not the rain. This is a serious rain event. But the winds are moving south and west of us. For a closer look, let's go to the map.

steak

○ ○ ○ ○ ○ ○ ○ ○ ○

The electricity was already out.

The Harris Teeter had power running off of a generator, though. It was a huge grocery store. People called it the Taj Ma Teeter. At timed intervals, sprays of cold mist would waft onto the produce from miniature, hidden nozzles. It was the only place in Lystra to buy the *New York Times*. It had good olives.

Evelyn Graham was rattling a grocery cart across the floor. She looked like Alexander Hamilton, tall and gaunt with a huge mass of grey hair frozen with Aqua Net. She wore jeans and a raincoat but usually went out in one of her black dresses, the ones that she wore to the funerals. They framed her long, pale neck in high contrast, making her head blossom like some withered cotton ball shooting out of a burnt stem. Evelyn went to almost all the funerals in Lystra, whether she knew the people or not. She lived alone, was still in good health, and she had a lot of free time, so she filled it up with funerals. She wasn't the only one; there were others who went to see and be seen, to feel like they were still part of the community. To Evelyn and the others, these funerals were social events whose invitations were printed daily in the *News & Observer* obituaries. There were no funerals today, though, because of the weather.

In central North Carolina, people really only mobbed the grocery if snow was forecast. But even though Hurricane Hugo hadn't hit Lystra dead on that morning, the electricity was out, so things were busy. Evelyn saw many people she knew. Leanne Vanstory was at the meat counter. Jesse Darren was buying batteries. She saw Welborne Ray rolling an empty shopping cart into the aisle beside her. It was the canned food and condiments aisle. He had on a suit that was not the one he'd worn last Tuesday, at the funeral for Mary Anne Hassel, but it was similar. He was always in a pinstriped suit. It looked like he had come from his law office, she thought. They had probably closed when the power went off.

Evelyn entered the pet food and paper products aisle. Through a thin stack of Charmin she heard Welborne Ray's voice.

"Not bad!" he was saying. "Good to see you."

"You too!" said another man. "Can't go four feet in here without seeing a familiar face."

Evelyn could not place the other voice, high and phlegmy, but she knew she recognized it from somewhere.

"I meant to say hi at Mary Anne's service the other day," Welborne said. "But I lost you."

"Ah. Shingles?" the voice said. "Who gets shingles?"

"More people than you think. My own mother had it before she passed."

"Mmm." There was a moment of silence. "I did see you there, talking to my neighbor."

Christ almighty, Evelyn thought. It's Van Lipsitz.

"Evelyn Graham? The old president?" Welborne said.

"God knows," Lipsitz said.

"Why is she at every funeral I go to? I mean, every single one."

"I know."

"She doesn't even know these people," Welborne said.

"I heard she told Amelia Hassel that her braces looked nice."

"No."

"At her own cousin's funeral. Pointed out her braces."

"Lord, I missed that."

"The poor girl was in tears."

"What can you say?" Welborne said. "I guess she's just lonely."

steak

"Amelia?"

"Evelyn. Peter's been dead for what? A decade? God, has it been a decade?"

Twelve, Evelyn thought. Twelve years.

"And who does she spend time with? Ruth Lingle?"

"Keep your voice down," Lipsitz said. "I think I just saw Ruth come in."

They were quiet for a moment. Evelyn looked around for Ruth.

Finally Welborne spoke again. "Look, I need some batteries before they're all gone. Good to see you, Van. Hope you don't wash away."

Evelyn wanted them to see her, to know that they weren't getting away with anything by talking about her right there in the Harris Teeter. She pushed her cart down the aisle and around the corner, up into the tunnel of ketchup and soy sauce. Welborne Ray had already walked off to look for his batteries, but Van Lipsitz was still there. He was lying on the ground with a broken jar of mustard exploded on the linoleum beside him, convulsing. One arm slid back and forth across the yellow puddle.

Evelyn rushed to him and fell onto her knees.

"Help!" she said. "Hey! Hey! There's a man here! Hey!"

She felt light from the fear and excitement. Euphoric. The deli man rounded the bend, sliding across part of the waxed floor as he ran.

⌐ ⌐ ⌐

Van Lipsitz's house was on the corner, beside Evelyn's and between hers and Mankin Park. He was divorced and wore large rimless glasses. What hair he had was white and combed over his shining crown. He was one of the few Jewish men in Lystra, and he worked for Jefferson Pilot Insurance. To Evelyn, he always seemed nice enough. They would see each other and wave, talk about the city's leaf pickup in the fall or how the squirrels were eating out of the bird feeders. He was a benign presence, almost invisible. Until he built the wall.

It was a brick wall around his backyard, a wall that blocked Evelyn's view of Buffalo Creek and the park. She had gone through hell trying to get him not to build it. She had brought it to the neighborhood council. It lowered her property value, decreased her quality of life, and so on. Still, Van Lipsitz had built the wall. He even had Welborne Ray represent him. Welborne had told the council that the wall was for safety, that it would keep the dog in. That Van lived alone, and that his dog was his best friend. He'd actually gotten Van to say that to the neighborhood council: "This dog is my best friend." Afterwards, after he had the approval, Van left two twelve-foot sections out of the wall, filling the gaps with chain link instead. Through these gaps, Evelyn could still see the creek.

Van had done this as a concession, one not even stipulated by the council. It didn't change the fact that Evelyn was livid, overwhelmed by the idea that her own neighbor would erect a seven-foot brick wall that, although ostensibly around his own yard, was also around hers. Or at least around a third of it. And it was the most important third, she thought. The side that gave her the view of Buffalo Creek, of Mankin Park, the park where she used to walk with her husband, where her children always tried to sled in the muddy aftermath of even the slightest flurry, where she had once even seen a salamander get snatched up by an albino owl, and where she never consciously thought about gazing until after the wall was built. "And make no mistake," she'd told anyone who would listen, "The view is not the same through chain link." She hadn't spoken to Van Lipsitz since. That had been ten years before she found him in the mustard.

steak

   ◦   ◦   ◦

Evelyn was tenderizing a skirt steak on her chopping block. She hit it hard and loud. She'd pulled it from the freezer earlier that morning, when the electricity had first gone out. The refrigerator had begun to thaw, and the steak hadn't been cheap. She didn't remember exactly how long it had been there, but it couldn't just sit out. She might as well have it for lunch.

The phone was still working, and Evelyn had it wedged between her shoulder and ear, the spiral yellow cord stretching taut across the room.

"He could have died," she was saying. "He's still in the hospital, you know. He still might."

Ruth Lingle was on the other end. She was a friend from Forbis and Dick Funeral Home. She worked there, in the business office. Evelyn knew her only from going there so often.

"This is going to sound silly," Ruth said. "But are you sure it was a seizure?"

"That's what the, um."

"EMT?"

"Yes. What the EMT said."

"And you found him. Can you believe? Of all people."

"I don't think of myself as a hero, really," Evelyn said. She thudded the mallet into the meat and a piece of something shot up, into her left eye. She squeezed her eyes shut and set the mallet down, then just stood there with her eyes closed and her head thrown back.

"Did you really just say that?" Ruth said.

"What? Yes. He's still in the hospital, you know. Hasn't been home yet. What a day."

"Don't think of yourself as a hero. I cannot believe you said that. What—"

The phone line went dead. Evelyn opened her eyes and walked to the wall. She hung the receiver on its mount. It was to the left of the refrigerator, which was covered in photographs. Photographs of her family. Photographs of her dead husband, Peter, who had been a realtor for RE/MAX. It had been a heart attack. Not unexpected. There was a picture of him whale watching. He just stood above the water in a yellow parka, a railing behind him, his face round and splotchy. He was giving a double thumbs-up. There were photos of her children at all ages, from birth till now, the two daughters thirty-six and thirty-nine and living in Charlotte. She was surrounded by these shiny, smiling faces. And her eyes were welling up, just a little. It was from the piece of meat in her eye, though. It was just meat in the eye.

Though the electricity and the phone lines were still out, it was becoming clear that the storm was veering further west than originally forecast. Evelyn's battery-operated radio was on and the weatherman was listing windspeeds and rainfall totals when a champagne Grand Marquis with a spiral antenna on the back pulled up to the curb. Welborne Ray stepped out in a trench coat. Evelyn saw him from the living room. She got up and walked to the door, grabbing an umbrella before stepping onto her stoop. When the umbrella opened, only one side billowed up, the other limp and dangling like a broken wing.

"Welborne!" she said, walking towards him. The umbrella wasn't keeping her very dry, the broken part whipping around in the wind.

"Hello," Welborne said. He was just standing in the rain at the curb, looking at Van Lipsitz's house.

"Do you know how he is?" Evelyn said. Welborne had gone with Van in the ambulance.

"Not well. Not well at all," he said. His eyes scanned the house. "It was a stroke."

"Oh my God," Evelyn said. "I didn't know you could have a seizure with a stroke."

"I don't know. I guess you can," Welborne said. He was spinning a huge gold ring around his index finger. "Ben asked me to come over and see if the house is alright. Make sure there isn't a tree through the roof or anything."

Evelyn thought of Ben, Van's sister, round and short and dumpy in her sweat suits. She was named after their father. She'd named her daughter the same, and most of Lystra had forgotten long ago that this was strange or even funny. People were used to it. If there was a family name that hadn't been used, sometimes it didn't matter what sex the child was.

They looked at the house together, rain overflowing the clogged gutters. It was a nice house, in the nicest neighborhood in Lystra, really, and Evelyn was struck by how similar Van's was to hers. It had been a long time since she'd looked at the two in this way. Of course, they were similar in construction, built by the same builder at the same time. They both had rhododendrons along the brick walkway, and throughout the two yards, the same plants were blooming, the same ones wilting.

"All looks well from here," Welborne said. He stepped forward. "I'm going to check the back."

Evelyn stepped along with him. She wanted to see the back of the house, too. She had never been on the other side of the wall.

The gate was permanently open, the wooden door removed long ago, and they walked along the shadowed side of the wall. It blocked the rain that was blowing in at an angle.

The dog that Van had originally built the wall for had been a golden retriever named Molly. She had died only one year after construction was complete. Until the wall was built, Molly had always stayed inside. Evelyn would see her only when Van walked her after work. But once the wall came up, Evelyn saw Molly all the time, through the sections of chain link. It had taken a while for her to warm up to that dog, but eventually, Evelyn began giving scraps to her through the chain link, but only when Van was at work. Molly would bark and rub against the fence, little tufts of fur pulling out when they got caught in the crossed wire. This had been close to nine years ago, so it was a surprise when Evelyn and Welborne stepped into the backyard and clearly heard a dog bark.

It was a skinny white pit bull smelling around the dryer vent. It looked up at them and barked again.

"Easy, boy," Welborne said.

The dog looked sick and mean. Evelyn grabbed Welborne's arm.

"Calm down, Evelyn," Welborne said.

The dog stepped towards them, growling. They backed into the shadowy space between the house and the wall, a narrow suburban alley. The dog stopped and watched them retreat. Evelyn dropped her wounded umbrella. She wished the gate had still been there to close.

Back in the front yard, Evelyn said, "Is that Van's dog?"

"He hasn't had a dog since Molly," Welborne said. "It must have just wandered over from somewhere."

He held his umbrella high above the two of them now, but Evelyn's back was still getting soaked.

"Here," he said, and gave her his arm. She took it in her hand, for the second time in moments. These two connections with Welborne's body felt like the first she'd had with a man in years. She knew that it wasn't true, that she had touched men. She'd shaken hands, she'd patted shoulders. She'd given countless hugs at funerals, to people she didn't even know. She'd even picked a piece of lint off the mailman's face once. But Welborne's giving his forearm to her, it felt different. It felt like Peter, her husband.

They walked slowly across Evelyn's lawn. The ground was so wet that their feet sunk in at each step.

"I'll call Animal Control," Welborne said.

"The phone's out."

She could hear their footsteps squishing in the soil.

"Then just stay inside until he's gone. It won't be long."

"Are you going back to the hospital?"

"I'm going to tell them this place hasn't floated away, and then I'm going to check on my own house. I'll be back this afternoon."

"That's just silly," Evelyn said. "I can keep an eye on the house."

Her front steps were mossy brick and became slick in the rain, so Evelyn held on to Welborne tightly as they ascended them.

"Are you sure it won't be awkward?" Welborne said at the top. "I know how things have been."

The umbrella caught the wind and pulled his arm up in a small sudden jerk.

"Been? It's been ten years," Evelyn said. "And it's just stupid. I don't care about the damn wall anymore."

She hadn't planned to say this, but as the words came out she felt them to be true.

Welborne cast his gaze downward.

"Well, great," he said. "Really. That's good to hear."

"No, really. Even when he built it. I thought I cared about it, but I didn't. I don't know. I don't know what's wrong with me. Even when I brought it to the neighborhood council, I . . ." Evelyn shook her head. Her back was very wet now. Water was dripping into her jeans. "I haven't been a good neighbor."

Welborne shook his head slowly.

"Evelyn, come on now. Come on. Stop that. Stop."

"No, I . . ."

"What's important is what you've said. You're over it. That's great."

"I told him he had ruined my life. I told him that Christians wouldn't do this to a neighbor. I . . ."

"Oh, Evelyn."

"What is wrong with me? I know how you think about me. I heard you at the grocery store."

Welborne looked into her eyes. He had to look up because she was taller than he was. His glasses were foggy.

"I am so sorry," he said. "We were just being rude, Evelyn."

"I have to dry off," Evelyn said. "I'm soaking." She nodded towards Van Lipsitz's house. "I'll keep an eye on it. Tell Ralph that I'll call if anything happens. I'm sorry to talk so much."

"No, no. Really," Welborne said. The umbrella jerked his arm up again.

That was when Evelyn's broken umbrella, the one that she'd dropped, came flapping out of Van Lipsitz's yard and flew across the street. She let go of Welborne's arm.

Inside, the battery-powered radio was still on. It made her nervous, because the reports were all about how Charlotte was getting the brunt of the storm. She was worried about Alison and Andrea, her two girls there.

From time to time, Evelyn could see the white dog cross by the section of chain link, sniffing at dark corners near the garage and around the hedges.

She went into the kitchen to see if the phone was still out. It was. The steak was soaking in Worcestershire sauce and the smell made her salivate. It was wrapped in tinfoil on the counter. She walked to it and lowered her nose. The smell was so strong that it made her nose burn. It was going to be a wonderful lunch.

She thought about Van Lipsitz. When he came back, she was going to talk to him. It was going to be easy now. It's always the first contact that is the hardest, she thought, and just being near him today at the Harris Teeter made her feel as if that first hurdle was over with. She'd saved his life!

Outside, the dog quit searching for whatever it was looking for and just lay down under the magnolia tree. It looked tired and resigned.

Evelyn went into the kitchen. The dog could have that steak. She didn't care. It wasn't too good for a dog.

She lifted the steak out of the saucepan and Worcestershire sauce dripped across the counter. She shook it over the sink, then walked down the dark hall.

Outside, the dog sat up and barked halfheartedly. Evelyn had forgotten to put a jacket on and her blouse was still soaking. The rain was pelting through the thin fabric, and by now her bra was even visible, but she didn't care. Who was going to see her?

The dog got up and ran towards the chain link, jumping against it. He was breathing heavily, his nose twitching to one side. His little front-foot pads pushed against the chain link, the crooked toenails reaching through the gaps.

Evelyn threw the steak into the air. It didn't clear the top of the fence, though, and bounced back, landing in the grass on her side. The dog whimpered and raked his nose across the metal.

"OK, OK," she said.

She leaned down to pick up the steak. It still smelled great.

Her head was less than a foot away from the dog's and he was whining. His tail was going so fast that it wagged his whole body. Saliva and rain dripped off of his jowls. Some of his white fur was stuck in the chain link, and it made Evelyn think about Molly. How sometimes Molly would do the same thing, how excited she'd be to see Evelyn. How she'd cry for the food. How she'd smell the scraps from across the yard and run.

"I know you want it," Evelyn said. "I know, boy. I know."

She threw the steak again and this time it arced over the fence, through the rain, and as it did the dog jumped, following it with his eyes, his nose, even his tongue. It was as if his previous lack of energy had been an act and some reserve had suddenly kicked in. Evelyn kept her arm outstretched as the dog hovered in the air, as that steak flew from her hand and into Van Lipsitz's yard, over that twelve-foot section of chain-link fence. As it cleared the wall.

The dog caught it in midflight and then started shaking it. Evelyn remembered that her father had explained to her, when she was a girl, that animals did this to kill their prey. Then the dog held the steak down with one paw and pulled off a stringy piece. He didn't chew it at all before he swallowed, though, and then he stretched his neck out, pointing his snout towards the fence. He opened his mouth wide and started plugging his tongue into the air, a clogged wheezing coming through his nose. He was choking.

Evelyn ran to her front yard and slid on the grass. She landed on her hip, and water immediately soaked through her pants from the grass. After a moment of panic, she got back up and limped into Van's yard, through the opening in the wall. The dog had turned and was facing her now, still doing the same thing with his mouth.

She grabbed his upper jaw with one hand, then stuck the other into his mouth. She felt the teeth and the sharp ridges on the roof of his mouth as her hand slid into his throat. She could get her middle finger and thumb deep in there, but she couldn't find anything. The dog sat down and Evelyn pulled her hand out. He

steak

collapsed onto his front paws and Evelyn knelt in the grass. Mud and water coated almost every inch of her pants now. She pried his jaws open again. He was completely docile, almost unconscious. She looked into his mouth, but there was nothing she could see. She didn't know if the Heimlich maneuver would work on a dog, but it was the only thing she even remotely knew how to do in this situation. She felt silly as she got around the back of the dog and put her hands under his rib cage and yanked.

The piece of steak landed in the grass and the dog burst into a spasm of coughing. Evelyn kept her arms around his torso and held him as he began to retch. Frothy yellow bile poured onto the dog's front legs and into the wet grass. She could feel him breathing now, jagged short breaths that shook his torso. The sensation of another life in her arms seemed suddenly profound and rare, and she did not want it to end. The thought then occurred to her that he might again become aggressive—he might not understand that she was trying to help. This was when he turned his dogface to her, strings of drool and rain dangling off his jowls. She held on to him, though, looking him in the face, unsure of what might happen next, feeling his heart beat like a trapped hummingbird, fluttering small and furious.

thawing

Cliff and Matthew had come for the dough.

"I'll go in," Matthew said. "But when I yell, open up. We can't leave it open or else all the cold air will come out."

He opened the door to the walk-in freezer and cold air swelled over Cliff, making his damp suit suddenly heavy and sharp. It smelled like flour and apricots. Matthew's flashlight cut across the inside of the freezer, lighting sheet pans with rows of cookie dough mounds, blue plastic buckets on the floor, cardboard boxes, and a three-tier yellow wedding cake with white flowers. The thick metal door then squeezed the light into a sliver before closing it in with the cold.

"Wait. Hey!" Matthew yelled, muffled through the freezer door.

Cliff pulled on the handle, but the door would not open.

"It's locked!"

"It's not locked! Pull!"

"I am!"

"Pull hard!" Matthew yelled. Cliff could barely hear him. "It seals up!"

Cliff pulled as hard as he could and the door finally released with a loud and low suck. Matthew stood with the flashlight beam on the top of his Adidas.

"Come in here real quick."

Cliff stepped inside.

"Let it close."

The door made its soft connection behind him, a solid, airtight seal. It was so cold Cliff felt his heart might stop. The flashlight beam reflected upwards from the floor, making Matthew's thin neck glow under the dark point of his chin. His moustache cast a strange shadow upwards that made it appear much thicker, as if it were growing up and into his nostrils.

"Birdie come in?" Matthew said.

Birdie, Cliff thought. Her name. He said, "She's still in the truck."

"You get in there?"

"In the truck?"

"No, in Birdie."

"I don't know."

Birdie managed this bakery. She was the girl Cliff had met at Tanfastic. When Matthew had offered to drive her home, she had asked if they would help her save her dough instead. Without electricity at the bakery, it was going to rise.

"She get you to use one of those ribbed condoms?" Matthew said. "Don't hold out on me, cuz. She loves those things, right?"

Cliff said, "Yeah." But he didn't know.

"That's what I thought," Matthew said, nodding. "We used to date. A couple, three, four years ago. Here." He handed Cliff a box of dough. "She's always been into those."

Cliff loaded four cardboard boxes of frozen cinnamon rolls into the camper top of Matthew's pickup. Birdie was in the cab of the truck, the back of her head a dark outline against the light. The thought that she had used a ribbed condom with Matthew was almost unbearable. Matthew was thirty and married. Had been for years. Birdie turned and smiled through the steamy glass. Cliff could hardly believe she had allowed him to touch her.

When they got into the truck she said, "You guys smell like cinnamon."

"Yeah," Matthew said.

"I could just eat you up."

They drove away from town, water spitting onto Cliff's face through a poor seal on the side window. The houses became more and more spread out, as if the land between each were swelling in the rain. Cliff watched Birdie for any special attention to Matthew. He exhausted all of his courage in maneuvering his hand close to hers, then finally launched it upon her tiny hand. She gripped him back and Cliff was suddenly invincible, completely satisfied and safe.

"That dough's Danish," Birdie said. "But we order it from France."

"How do they keep it frozen from over there?" Matthew said.

"Same as fish," Birdie said, and looked at Cliff like he would understand. He smiled. "It's the only dough in the bakery that I don't make myself. It's for cinnamon buns."

"Where're we taking it?" Cliff said.

"Oh man," Matthew said. "Wait till you see this guy's house."

"Gordon," Birdie said.

"He's got a generator because he's crazy? And only crazy people have generators?" Matthew said, messing with the windshield wipers. When he was distracted, all of his sentences sounded like questions. He couldn't find the right speed in the variant rain. "And he's got a deep freezer for hunting stuff? Anyway, we always go out there during Christmas, to look at his lights. He just puts up ridiculous amounts of Christmas lights. This guy. He raised a calf inside, in his kitchen, once. He actually put hay down and closed the room off. He used to have peacocks, too. I don't know what happened to them. You're going to love it."

"I had to give him Mr. Bojangles," Birdie said to Matthew. She turned to Cliff. "My old bloodhound."

"Was he a puppy?" Cliff said.

"No. But he was eating our furniture and stuff. Rebecca even put Tabasco on the legs of the kitchen table so that he wouldn't eat it. But he ate it. Stewart has all this land and does the fox hunt, so we gave him to him."

They turned onto a road straddled by wide, low tobacco fields. It was the first expansive view Cliff had had since arriving in Lystra the night before. Everywhere else was shaded by low limbs drooping under the burden of weather. Here, the sky was suddenly broad and dark over huge tobacco leaves, pressed low to the ground, swelling in waves as gusts of wind pushed across the fields. Rivulets of water ran between each row and as they drove by, the lines of crops seemed to fan out from one mysterious point on the horizon. As Matthew sped up, the rows clicked by in a blur, only the vanishing point remaining consistent beside them.

As Cliff held Birdie's hand, every song that played on the radio was suddenly poignant. Each had at least one verse that could have been written for them and them alone. The soft country music came in low until they reached a varied garden patch with strings of multicolored Christmas lights strung across the ground between the rows, lighting it up like a dozen miniature landing strips. After not seeing electricity for over an hour, the glow was a revelation.

Matthew turned off the radio and said, "Guess he left them up."

They turned into a gravel driveway with a line of grass down the middle. Fifteen or more cars were parked along the way. A white plantation house with a new blue tin roof stood at the end. Three windows on the first floor glowed with electric light. On the porch a hand-painted piece of scrap wood said BEWARE OF CAT! above a childlike painting of a black cat with green eyes and a yellow mouth full of bared fangs. Below the cat was the inscription MAMMA. Classical piano music issued dully through the walls.

thawing

Matthew rang the doorbell and the door opened almost imme-diately. The piano overture intensified. Inside stood a woman with grey hair in a tight ponytail, wearing a crisp black skirt suit and holding a glass of red wine. Her hair was pulled so tightly across her scalp that Cliff wondered if it hurt.

"Hi," Matthew said. "I hope we're not interrupting anything. Is Gordon here?"

"Yeaaahillllshowyoo," the woman said. She then slowly took a piece of ice out of her mouth and dropped it into the wine.

"Matthew," Matthew said. "Joel and Mary Anne's son."

"Prissy." Prissy didn't look as if she had any idea who Matthew's parents were.

He gestured to Birdie and Cliff and said, "And everyone."

Prissy led them into the kitchen, where an older man in a white tracksuit drank wine from a jar. A woman wearing a long tie-dyed shirt over black spandex shorts was taking pictures of him with a large camera. When they entered, she turned it on them and said, "Youth!" and the flash went off.

"This is Matthew and everyone," Prissy said.

"You guys live in the red house?" said the man in the white track-suit. He was looking at Cliff.

"I live in Chattanooga," Cliff said.

The man shrugged, then held out a bedraggled, drooping cigarette.

"It's grown on the premises," he said.

Cliff didn't smoke, but Birdie took a drag and passed it to him. He knew that people didn't do that with actual cigarettes. He was regressing in levels of risk taking. He could still feel the cocaine. He tried to do exactly what Birdie had done, inhaled, and then coughed a little. It must have been a marijuana cigarette. Prissy then led them through a dark, narrow hallway lined with mounted deer, their sable necks reaching out from the shadowed plaster.

The living room was filled with people, many more than Cliff would have expected even from the number of cars. Most were well dressed, men in suits, women in pearls. Cliff thought that these people must have dressed for work before learning that their places of employment were closed. For the first time in hours he felt comfortable in his own suit. A low cloud of cigarette smoke hung above twos and threes throughout the expansive room. The classical music was loudest here, a melody that Cliff recognized from a commercial for diamonds.

A large man in a dark suit turned towards them as they entered. He wore a red tie with a white triangle in the center, and his hair, though gone on top, was pulled from the sides into a small, greasy ponytail.

"Gents," he said.

"Hey, Gordon," Matthew said. "We need to freeze some dough."

"You mean *dough* dough?"

"Yeah, like actual dough."

"You know I have a deep freezer."

"Yeah. That's what I'm saying."

"Splendid," Gordon said, then seemed to notice Birdie for the first time. He pursed his lips and brought his eyebrows together. "Sweetie," he said. "It's been a long time since I've seen you." He grimaced.

"What?"

"I don't know how to say this."

Then he didn't say anything. He just shook his head and continued to grimace.

"What?" Birdie said.

He kept shaking and grimacing. Finally he said, "Your dog is in the freezer."

thawing

Cliff felt like the top of his head was lifting off of his skull. He guessed the marijuana cigarette was working. He felt like he had been drugged, and then, when he thought about it further, realized that he was, in fact, drugged.

"A man brought him to the door on Independence Day and there wasn't a mark on him," Gordon continued. "It looked like he'd been hit by a pillow."

"He's in the freezer?" Birdie said.

Gordon nodded. "We stuff them all." He put his hand on Birdie's shoulder. "Burying an animal is weird, too, if you think about it."

Cliff couldn't believe what he was hearing. After a moment of stunned silence, Stewart then turned to him.

"Young man," he said, laying a heavy hand on Cliff's shoulder. He bent to Cliff's level and squinted. "I believe you've become a Chinaman."

"What?" Cliff said.

"You can barely open your eyes."

Cliff tried to lift his eyelids and Gordon chuckled lightly, then began to lead them through the house. People were everywhere. One room was filled with vintage pinball machines and people activating their flippers. Lights and buzzers and bells sounded in a cacophony of carnival joy. Gordon opened a pale green umbrella before leading them to a small barn in the rear of the property. The roofline of the building was decorated in more Christmas lights and inside was one deep freezer like a large white refrigerator tipped onto its side. When Gordon lifted its lid, mist rolled out like some Halloween prop. As the mist cleared, Cliff looked down at one of the largest dogs he had ever seen. It was curled onto its side, seemingly asleep. But its dappled coat of browns was covered in a thin layer of crystalline ice, making it glimmer in the freezer light, accentuating the massive topography of muscle. This dog wasn't waking up. There were more animals, too. Ferrets. Cats. Squirrels. One black cat was enclosed in the kind of plastic baggie that had one yellow and one blue edge so that when properly sealed, the colors combined to form a green confirmation of freshness. The green line ran across the cat's folded ears and diagonally down its back. Cliff suddenly thought this must be Mamma, from the porch's warning sign.

"I believe there should be room," Gordon said. "Just put it on top? Splendid."

When Cliff and Matthew returned from the truck with two boxes apiece they found Birdie alone, gazing into the open freezer. She languidly moved out of the way as they approached, as if an invisible thread had been attached to her hips and gently pulled.

"You OK?" Matthew said, setting the dough on the ground.

She buried her face into Matthew's sternum and Cliff tried not to panic. He thought, I should have asked her first. Matthew patted her head and said, "He had it good out here. I mean, you see this place?" Birdie kept her face buried in his chest. "This was the good life."

Cliff thought again of the ribbed condom.

"Fuck!" Birdie said, pulling her face away and wiping her eyes. "I get like this when I'm high." Then she looked at the freezer and said, "He should at least, like, bury him. You don't . . . You *bury* them!"

"There's nothing left but the clothes there, sweetie. Nothing but the clothes."

"We shouldn't have ever ever ever let him come out here."

Cliff felt like he had to do something. But he could think of nothing to do except put his boxes of dough into the freezer. He gingerly placed the first box atop Bojangles, but the last one wouldn't fit. He tried to wedge it between Mamma Cat and a ferret, but there was simply too much dough.

"Here, cuz," Matthew said, taking the box from Cliff.

Cliff was glad when Matthew also failed. He placed the box on the hay-strewn floor.

"Can we let one slide?" Matthew said.

"That's forty bucks," Birdie said. She looked at Cliff expectantly, her wide-set eyes red.

"What about the kitchen?" Matthew said.

She raised her eyebrows and turned, then Matthew picked up the box and they jogged into the rain. Cliff stayed in the barn, paralyzed with jealousy. Finally he returned to the freezer and lifted a box of dough. Bojangles' expansive whiskered lips still appeared damp, as if they might at any moment leak a fresh string of frothy slobber. Cliff took the other boxes out and set them on the floor.

There had been only a few moments in Cliff's life like this one. There was the first time he got the courage to climb into bed with Rebecca. The time he stole third in the county baseball playoffs. The time he wrote a love poem for Shirley Ronconi and actually gave it to her. It was suddenly clear that there had been few moments of actual courage in his young life. He leaned into the freezer in that dark and foreign barn and felt the same rush as he had when that ball had closed the void between him and the third baseman, when his flesh had stuck to Rebecca's with aloe. The ridge of the chest was cold across his stomach as he wrapped his arms around Bojangles. The animal smelled faintly of cheese. Cliff began to drag him against the side of the freezer, pulling until the body rolled over the side. Bojangles was heavier than he had guessed, and Cliff lost control. The dog landed with one of its legs perpendicular to the floor and when it connected, it popped loudly as it broke.

Cliff began to drag the dog across the floor. Outside, the broken leg wavered like a loose rudder across the wet gravel. Cliff struggled to lift the body into the open tailgate of Matthew's truck. A blue tarp was wadded into the corner. Cliff tucked its sides under the dog and pushed the blue bundle far into a corner.

When Matthew and Birdie returned, Matthew was still holding the extra box of dough. There'd been no room. He said, "We're going to cook it."

Back in the truck, Cliff watched the phantom vanishing point at the back of the tobacco field as it traveled beside them again, its constant fan of tobacco rows still expanding and spinning by. He feared that Bojangles might slide into the rearview, but the trip was uneventful until they reached one plot of land near Birdie's house that had been cleared of its crop. As they sped along its edge, a white dog suddenly appeared atop the muddy mounds of harvested earth. The animal bounded slowly and gracelessly across the stubble of stalks like a white moth staggering through a thick cloud of smoke. Cliff thought it might be a vision, some pale dog spirit trailing Bojangles. Maybe it was the marijuana cigarette. He didn't know. It gave him chills, though, even after the field and its ghost dog disappeared as the truck hurried past more tobacco and then down Birdie's driveway.

Cliff lined frozen cinnamon rolls on a sheet pan at the kitchen table while Birdie sprinkled cinnamon. They worked by candlelight, cooking the extra dough while the rain continued against the windowpanes, lower pitched here than in the bakery but no less urgent. The dough was already fleshy and swollen, the yeast coming to life as its temperature rose. Cliff was proud of his exact rows, his role in the creation. Birdie intended to take the finished rolls to Rebecca's wedding, now moved from its original location, Mankin Park, to a haphazard fete at Matthew's house later that evening. In the corner, a large metal mixing bowl with a towel wrapped around

thawing

it caught a constant flow of brown water that was trickling out of a rotten spot of plaster on the ceiling.

The legs of the kitchen table were scarred with deep pale grooves. Cliff guessed this was Bojangles' work. He imagined Rebecca painting Tabasco onto those legs and it seemed ingenious, too clever for anyone to have come up with on their own. He wondered if she had read of it somewhere, and how many bottles it had required. Then he remembered that the trick had failed and was glad, because if it hadn't, perhaps the girls never would have given Bojangles to Gordon, and then he wouldn't have had the surprise now waiting in the truck.

Matthew washed his hands at the sink, then walked over to Birdie and Cliff and put a damp hand on the shoulder of each.

"I like you," he said. "And I like you. And I just want to say that I think it's a good thing that you two have kindled this little romance."

Birdie smiled and Cliff looked down, shaking his head.

"Hey, cuz," Matthew said. "There're no secrets here. Chill!" He shook Cliff's shoulder a little. "You know what cracks me up, though? He told me you're still into those ribbed condoms."

Cliff tried to remain calm. He took a deep breath and said, "No, I didn't."

"We're all friends," Matthew said.

Birdie turned towards Cliff, but he couldn't meet her gaze.

"I didn't," he said.

"No, it's alright," Birdie said.

"No, but I . . ."

"Yeah, I'm still into them," she said.

Cliff felt like he had never had so little at stake. What else could happen? So he stood up and said, "I'll be back."

The chill still radiated out of Bojangles' legs as Cliff pulled him from the truck. It was fascinating how one could so quickly improve at such a particular task, how his body could learn the odd choreography of moving this dead bloodhound. It was so much easier the second time. He propped the frozen torso on his shoulder and walked.

He reentered the kitchen and stopped a yard beyond the threshold, rain dripping out of his hair and into his eyes. The storm door slammed shut behind him. Bojangles' back leg, the one that was not broken, stood straight out, pointing at Birdie and Matthew as they washed their hands at the sink. Matthew turned from the sink, looking for a towel, when he saw Cliff.

"The fuck!" he said, stepping back. Frosting hung from his moustache. He held his hands before him like both had gone limp, water running off his drooping fingers onto the floor below. Birdie followed Matthew's gaze, then held her wet hands to her mouth in shock.

"It's so we could bury him," Cliff said.

Matthew and Birdie just silently stared. The chill from Bojangles had seeped into Cliff's shoulder and he thought, What if I have to take him back?

"Cliff!" Matthew finally said, and laughed one loud, hoarse guffaw. "Holy crap!"

Birdie took her hands away from her face and revealed her gap-toothed smile.

"That is the most fucked up thing I have ever seen in my life," Matthew said.

"You," Birdie said, "are crazy."

But Cliff could tell she didn't mean it. What she really meant was something like thank you.

He dug a wide, shallow grave in Birdie's backyard, which filled with red mud at each shovelful, then went inside to retrieve the corpse.

thawing

He resisted Matthew's offers to help, insisting again on carrying the dog himself. He felt strong, like some righteous minister leading his flock to the service. He gingerly laid Bojangles in the grass at the edge of the hole. His back ached and his blistered hands stung, but Birdie's dog was going to be buried and she was going to have him to thank for it. He felt good. He had crossed a milestone of courage, of boldness. He didn't care that by now his parents were surely panicking, looking for him in the storm. This was more important.

He stood back and admired his work, then turned to the mourners. But Matthew and Birdie were backing up, both faces filled with silent terror. Cliff followed their gaze. It was a white dog, the same he had seen crossing the field of mud, now standing by the rhododendron bush behind the grave like some canine angel come to hasten the process. As it approached, Cliff too retreated. The dog was a pit bull, a sick and thin one. Its ears were flattened, its tail hidden between its legs. Cliff looked to the others, unsure if this was some hallucination, perhaps a delayed marijuana-cigarette effect, but Birdie and Matthew were both stunned, clearly attuned to the same apparition.

"Not good," Matthew whispered.

"I saw it in the tobacco fields," Cliff said.

"Oh my God," Birdie repeated, so quietly Cliff could hear only *ga* cutting through the wind.

The dog began sniffing slowly around Bojangles, pausing predictably and yet unbelievably at the frozen anus.

Surely this phantom intruder would disappear in time, Cliff thought. They could just go inside and wait. But Cliff felt somehow proprietary about this moment, defensive of its fragile sanctity. He had gone too far to let this go.

"Hey!" he said, and stepped forward.

"Cliff!" Birdie cried, grabbing him from behind.

But the dog had already begun its attack. It rushed towards them across the wet grass so quickly that its paws barely touched the sagging blades beneath them. Birdie held on tightly, and suddenly the beast was upon them. Two white paws landed on Cliff's shoulders and a tongue with one black spot shaped like some unknown country shot into the space below his chin. Cliff clenched his eyes and held up a hand to ward off the teeth, but no teeth came—only that wet, urgent muscle. Cliff lifted his heavy eyelids and found no dog spirit, no attacking predator, only a stray, sick pit bull looking for sugar and cinnamon. He leaned back into Birdie's tiny arms and let the dog lick.

trampoline

Manny stood with his hands on the rusty frame of the trampoline. He was a tall, skeletal freak with huge lips and a blond pompadour that was now drooping in the rain. Leaves were blowing into him and sticking onto his arms. Heavy, fat raindrops splattered onto his forehead and down his neck.

The trampoline was big, probably six feet across, and circular. Manny picked up one side of it, then let it fall back onto the yard, and the rusty metal springs rattled.

He looked around for something to hide it with. There was an upturned three-speed bicycle with only one wheel. A charred grill in the high grass. There was a pile of plates there, too, which Manny had never noticed. Nothing that might help. The whole neighborhood was like this. Junk in unmowed yards. One-story brick houses. No sidewalks. No curbs.

Manny forced the trampoline onto its side. It wasn't heavy, and because the frame was round he could roll it. And so he began rolling it towards the street.

Manny had been excited when Amelia had woken him up that morning, because it was the first time she'd spoken to him since Friday. It soon became clear, however, that she was only yelling at him about the trampoline in the yard. A trampoline where there had never been a trampoline before.

Amelia was Manny's girlfriend. She was little, twenty-seven years old, with stringy brown hair and a mouth that always looked dark and chunky because of the set of braces she had recently been fitted with. She'd been living with Manny in the house there on Boylan Avenue since they graduated from high school.

The reason she hadn't been talking to him the past few days was because of what had happened with Casper.

Casper was the white pit bull Amelia had recently found.

Manny hated the dog. He truly hated it. He didn't want it at all. He was embarrassed by it. The neighbors were scared of it. It barked at anything that moved. It loved going after squirrels, cats, moths, anything, but especially people whom it sensed were even slightly scared of it. On top of it all, Amelia made Manny walk it and pick up after it with little plastic baggies. It was a pit bull, Manny had tried to explain to her. "It's dangerous. It's like some redneck trophy bride."

On the previous Friday, while Amelia was at Elon, going to her nursing class, Manny had put Casper into his Chevy Cavalier and driven out to the spillway. He liked to walk out there, through the woods at the edge, where he didn't have to worry about the dog attacking anyone or pick up after it.

It was a sunny day and the shade felt good as he pulled into the little turnaround near the concrete lip. The gravel was stenciled with light through the branches. He opened the passenger-side door and Casper immediately sprinted out, crapping a huge, stinking mound on the gravel before chasing a squirrel across the clearing. Manny hadn't even had time to put the leash on. He called the dog's name, but each time Casper just ran a little bit farther. Manny didn't think the dog even knew its new name yet. They'd had it for only a few weeks. If the dog wanted to run away, so be it. Manny wasn't going to wait. This was his chance. So he quietly got back into his car and drove away, watching Casper in the rearview mirror licking the air and staring up at the branches.

trampoline

Amelia came home that afternoon and Manny told her what had happened. He said, "I've got bad news, baby."

She told him to go back. To go back and get the dog. Manny could see little pretzel pieces in her braces as she spoke.

"How the hell am I going to get the dog back?" he said. "He's gone. Gone. He ran away."

"Did he run into the spillway?"

"No, he didn't run into the spillway. Does it matter? He ran away by the spillway. Look. It was not safe having that dog here, Amelia."

"I cannot believe this."

"What? That thing's always showing up here anyway. Maybe he'll come back. I tried to catch him."

"Manny, I know you. I know you didn't try. Not really," she said. She was starting to tear up.

That was the first night he slept in the living room.

▭ ▭ ▭

The trampoline was surprisingly easy to roll, but Manny had no idea where to take it. He was just standing at the end of the drive-way, trying to think of where it might have come from. His friend Alec had helped him steal it the night before. Of this he was sure. And they had been very drunk. On many things. But beyond that, the specifics were gone. Clearly the trampoline was from a house nearby—they couldn't have moved it far.

Their neighbor Flash, the thirty-two-year-old newspaper deliveryman, was rolling up the windows of his white van at the curb. He had long blond hair that grew only from the sides of his head. It was pulled back into a thin, wet ponytail. Neither Manny nor Flash waved, even though both looked at the other.

"Hey, Flash!" Manny said. "Know whose trampoline this is?"

Flash looked at Manny with his mouth open. He shrugged.

"Thanks, pal! Just, you know, trying to sort this out."

A burst of wind threatened to force the trampoline over, but Manny leaned into it. The trampoline was like some suburban sail, straining to drag him along. The rain was overflowing the storm drains and he was already soaked. He turned towards where Boylan Street connected to Tripp Lane. This was the way he'd have come home the night before.

Across the street, Kenny Craven was on his front stairs under a camouflage umbrella. He was a young guy who always had sunglasses hanging around his neck and wore shorts no matter what the weather was. Manny never saw him do anything other than grill out by himself.

"Whatcha got there, Manny? Trampoline?"

"Yeah. Listen. Somebody put it in my yard last night. You know who might be missing a trampoline?"

"Hmm. Don't know. Hey, I heard this thing's going towards Charlotte," Kenny said, looking up at the sky. "Bummer."

"Right."

"I thought it was gonna be a big one."

"Yeah."

Manny continued to roll the trampoline.

"Hey, wait!" Kenny said. "Listen, if the power goes out, I'm going to be grilling up all these steaks I got in the freezer. I can't just let them go bad. You guys should come over."

Manny nodded. He was always avoiding Kenny's invitations.

Again the trampoline almost blew over. Manny kept it up.

Boylan Street was just a short dead end, one block long. There were about ten houses on the whole street. On its open end, Boylan continued down a little hill and connected to Tripp Lane. Manny kept rolling towards the hill, the rain and wind buffeting him. More leaves blew into his face and against the trampoline. He made it

trampoline

to the top of the hill and stopped rolling. Tripp was a larger street with more traffic and Manny knew he couldn't roll the trampoline down it. He also couldn't just leave it in the street. He stopped and just held it there, swaying in the wind.

"Hey!" Kenny said. He had stepped into the road behind Manny. "Set that thing down. Come here for a second."

Manny wiped at his dripping face. He didn't have any desire to enter Kenny's house, but he knew he couldn't return home with the trampoline. He was at a loss. With exaggerated arm motions, Kenny gestured for him to come in. So Manny turned around, set his shoulder, and started back up Boylan.

Kenny's front yard was one of the largest on the street and was empty except for a deflated volleyball melted halfway onto the ground, the high grass around it wet and drooping. Manny set the trampoline down by the curb, the springs rattling in assorted wavering pitches. As he walked through the high grass to the door, water from the thick vegetation seeped through the last dry spots on his pants.

"Power just went off," Kenny said. "So the cookout is *on*. I want you to look at these steaks."

Manny followed Kenny inside. The house was dark and smelled like cigarettes. Manny stood beside the kitchen window and wiped himself off with a dishrag. Someone had painted a large black wizard on the front of Kenny's refrigerator, where he was pulling huge, frosted pieces of wrapped meat out of the thawing freezer.

"We have to eat these *today*," Kenny said. "I'm putting them on ice, but that'll only last so long. Really. Pick one out." He held up a chuck blade. "Look at this."

Manny nodded. He was just stalling for time. He still couldn't think of anywhere to put the trampoline. He looked away, out the window, at two young boys who had suddenly appeared. They looked to be about nine or ten, both blond with shaggy bowl cuts, and stood silently beside the trampoline. One wore a green Izod shirt, the other a T-shirt with The Punisher on it. Manny had seen them before, at the end of the street, where they read comic books on the stoop of a house exactly the same as his.

"Hey, look," Manny whispered.

Kenny walked over with a set of ribs in his hand.

Without speaking to his friend, the boy in the Izod got onto the trampoline and began to jump. His hair slowly floated up with him on each bounce while drops of rain made spots of dark green on his shirt. He was doing at least twice his own height. More, actually. It was easy and slow, and then he did a perfect flip, his legs tucked beneath him as he languidly turned through the rain.

Manny was mesmerized, probably still partially drunk, but people truly couldn't normally jump this high, even on a trampoline.

"Think it's theirs?" Kenny said.

Manny hadn't thought of this.

He walked through the front hall and pushed the storm door open. Izod violently turned to him in midair.

"Hey," Manny called. "That your trampoline?"

Izod said, "School's *out*."

Then The Punisher said, "It's Myron's. They left it."

Manny vaguely remembered now. The Haskells, at the end of Boylan, had just moved. He remembered going through a pile of trash in their backyard the night before, ripping apart a Trapper Keeper while Alec put on an apron. He remembered breaking a long fluorescent lightbulb against a tree, then finding the trampoline in a dark corner of the yard. All of a sudden he felt free, released. Almost happy. This wasn't anybody's trampoline now.

"Let me on that thing," he said.

trampoline

Izod slid off quickly, spooked, wiping rust marks down the side of his shorts.

Manny swung his bony leg up onto the frame. He got himself into the middle and slid a bit in the rain, which was now coming down steadily. Then he began to bounce.

The Punisher started laughing.

"Yeah," Manny said.

He was clearing several feet and the trampoline creaked and rattled. His feet almost touched the grass each time he landed, the fabric sagging drastically beneath him.

"Amelia!" He knew she could hear him from across the street. "Amelia!"

As he rose in the air, before he had reached the top of his arc, he saw the screen door of his house swing open.

"I'm gonna flip!" Manny yelled, his hair an explosion. "Watch!"

He hit the bottom but his legs slipped out beneath him. He whipped back onto the fabric, his head just missing the metal frame. Then he rose back into the air for a second as he flew over the edge and crumpled to an electric stop on the wet grass.

Manny was sure that he had been broken. Completely. Every bone. He moved his legs. They moved. He did it again. They didn't even hurt. He did an internal assessment. There was nothing that actually hurt.

Rapid footsteps scurried across the grass. It was The Punisher, standing above him in terror. He was so wet that Manny could see his little boy nipples through the T-shirt.

"Are you OK?" The Punisher asked.

Manny looked across the street. Amelia was standing on the top step in a red raincoat.

Manny laid his head back and yelled, "Goddamn it! Oh Christ almighty. My leg! Oh God!"

"Oh my God. Lady," The Punisher said, turning to Amelia. Manny moaned.

Amelia slowly walked across the street and Kenny stepped outside.

"It's his leg!" Izod yelled.

Manny moaned again, then listened. The rain pinged off the trampoline.

"You alright, Manny?" Kenny said, kneeling down beside him.

"I . . . I think it's his leg, sir," Izod said to Kenny.

This gave Manny a new burst of energy and he began to moan again.

"Oh my God," The Punisher said, his voice cracking into a sob.

"Is this your trampoline?" Amelia said from the curb.

"It's Myron's," Izod said.

"Who is Myron?"

"He lived down there. They moved."

The Punisher was whimpering now.

"Manny," Amelia called. "You're scaring the children."

"I love you!" Manny yelled. "You're talking to me!"

She didn't say anything. Kenny was still kneeling beside him.

"My leg isn't really hurt!"

"I know it isn't," Amelia said.

"What the *fuck*?" Kenny said, standing up.

"Go home now, boys. Go on," Amelia said, walking away. "And Manny, take that thing back."

Manny heard four little Nikes scurry off. Then, after a moment, two screen doors slammed shut as Kenny and Amelia went back inside their houses.

He lay there for a long time, long enough that he began to feel as if both he and the ground around him were so saturated that he was melting into it. The rain had become a solid blanket pushing

trampoline

him into the soil. The wind was constant, just strong enough to force the weakest branches out of the dead oak at the edge of the yard. They landed with quiet thuds around him.

Manny rolled his head to one side and looked through the grass and fallen branches. Amelia had opened the windows to let the pressure out of the house.

He got up and pushed the trampoline back onto its side. A sheet of water fell off it in a rush. He began rolling it into the road.

Though Manny knew they'd moved out, the Haskells' house did not look uninhabited. There was still a plastic Big Wheel in the front yard and the garden had a hose strung across it. Wind chimes still hung from the gutter, emitting a constant, violent clanging. The air smelled electric.

He rolled the trampoline down the driveway. In the back there were scattered pieces of trash on the ground, things he hazily remembered from the night before. The apron, the Trapper Keeper. Old magazines and Tupperware. And a dog. A skinny, dirty dog sniffing in a torn bag of trash. A skinny, dirty white pit bull.

Manny let the trampoline down and it made its funny rattle.

Casper raised his close-set eyes and barked once, then went directly back to the trash.

God loves me, Manny thought.

Old boxes of food that were ripped apart formed a circle around Casper. Sloppy Joe mix. Jell-O. Beef bouillon cubes. Casper wasn't interested in Manny. It didn't matter, though. He had found his way back from five miles away in a hurricane. Casper was back, and Amelia was going to be very happy.

The rain was falling in huge sheets now and the wind began blowing in extended, violent bursts. The chimes flew off the gutter and landed with a last muffled clatter in the grass. Manny ran out to the street, leaving Casper to the trash. He had to get Amelia, show her that he'd put the trampoline back and found the dog. The luck, he thought. The luck!

He didn't have to go far. When he made it to the Haskells' front lawn, he saw Amelia standing in the road in front of their house. She was looking at the spot in Kenny's yard where Manny had been lying, where the trampoline had been. Now a large branch from their dead oak tree lay in the spot, its branches reaching up, long wet veins dripping black against the sky. Manny couldn't help but think Amelia had come back out to make sure he was alright, that the branch hadn't landed on him.

He jogged towards her and called out, "Amelia! Amelia!" then smiled when she looked at him. She looked furious, mad with confusion and fear.

"I'm OK," Manny said, coming up the middle of the empty street. "I'm right here. Right here."

He slowed to a stop and put his arms around her.

"I hate you," she said in a sob.

"I know, I know. But you'll be getting over that very soon."

A torn white trash bag was stuck on Casper's head. It was a strange sight, a white dog with a white bag over its head, barking and running in a slow, jerky circle. There was more trash scattered on the ground around Casper's shuffling paws.

Amelia pulled the bag off his head. Casper snapped at her hand and she stepped back. He barked twice, then crouched and bared his teeth.

"Casper," Manny said. "Casper!"

"He'll be alright once he gets some food," Amelia said. "Hey boy. Hey boody boody."

Casper hissed air through his teeth. Amelia's back was against the trampoline frame now. She had nowhere else to go.

trampoline

"My God," she said.

Manny took Amelia's hand in his own and put another at the small of her back. He stood between her and Casper, then helped her onto the trampoline, where Casper couldn't reach. She crawled up and sat in the middle. Manny followed her onto the undulating surface, then stood and helped her to her feet.

Casper carried on for another minute or so, then went back to chewing on an empty bag of gingersnaps.

At first Manny and Amelia tried to stand still on the trampoline, but the combination of two weights sent one up every time the other moved. And Manny kept on moving, taking steps and sort of bouncing without leaving the fabric. They stopped fighting the trampoline, finally, and just started jumping in this alternating rhythm.

They were each getting higher. Manny wondered if Amelia had ever done this before. She looked so comfortable. From time to time, he thought he even saw her smiling in the air.

The discarded trash bag had already filled with an overflowing puddle, and Casper was violently lapping from it. The wind was blowing trash around underneath them and the rain was exploding off the fabric at their feet. Manny's giant lips were floating up with his hair as Amelia's braces glittered darkly from her smile. They kept on bouncing like this, higher and higher, and for a moment every jump, as one fell and the other rose, each was suspended in air beside the other.

MIDDAY

*We're still seeing some serious flooding as rain
continues at record levels throughout the Piedmont
at this hour. Let's look at some footage shot from
around the viewing area.*

*This is in downtown Lystra a few hours ago. Look
at that.*

*And here's Mankin Park, also in Lystra. There's a
bridge under all that. Massive flooding in the Boylan
area there in Lystra.*

*Tragic scene in Alamance County at this hour.
This is by the Haw River in Graham, where flooding
has forced cattle onto the only dry space they can find.
That is the top of a barn.*

*And this is the Hagee Recycling Plant outside
Durham. They lost an area of roofing on their sorting
arena; therefore, I'm guessing that would be the newspaper area. Look at that.*

*Extensive flooding reported throughout the Raleigh-
Durham area at this hour, but we can expect some
clearing later in the day.*

For a clearer picture, let's go to the map. Rob?

humans fall into my field

⊝　⊝　⊝　⊝　⊝　⊝　⊝　⊝　⊝

In the parking lot behind his veterinary clinic, Dr. Pat Doublehead led Confetti through the floodwater. Pat had tied a lab coat around the horse's head, remembering that horses should be blindfolded during barn fire evacuations. He didn't know if that wisdom also applied to a flood, but Confetti was staying calm as they struggled through the knee-high water.

Pat had already evacuated the lizards, the cats, the dogs, and the rabbit, almost all of which had been boarded with him by evacuees from the coast or locals concerned that their own houses might flood. He had assured these pet owners that his office was safe. It never flooded. Not before Hurricane Hugo had blown in that morning. Now a sky that looked like mashed potatoes was dropping endless rain onto Lystra and the water was already into his file cabinets.

Pat was a paunchy forty-one-year-old Cherokee Indian whose weathered face lacked almost any chin. His bottom lip was full and red and stuck out over this chin void, framed by fat cheeks creased by a permanent smile. A bristle of thick black hair grew low on his forehead, under which Pat kept wiping at his pinched eyes as wind blew spray into them.

Close to three decades had passed since Pat had ridden bareback in Cherokee ceremonies at the reservation, but he thought he might still remember how. He threw his arms over the horse's spine and began to pull. He had almost reached the point where he could swing his right leg over Confetti's back when he slid off, into the water.

All of his weight bore down on his left wrist and something stabbed into his palm. When he lifted his hand out of the water, a long wooden splinter lay under the translucent flesh, probably three inches long, reaching from his pinkie to the meat before his thumb. It was thick and his hand was more numb than painful. It was the numbness that scared him.

Confetti hadn't moved; he just stood calm and blindfolded in the water. Pat began to climb the horse again. There were no other options. Pat's pickup truck stood behind them in even deeper water, its engine fatally submerged. This time he reached Confetti's back, where he untied the lab coat and tossed it into the water. The current carried it away, spinning like a drowning ghost, as Pat and Confetti began to walk.

⚬ ⚬ ⚬

Confetti was a twenty-seven-year-old roan who belonged to Pat's sister, Wendy. Wendy and Pat were the last full-blooded Cherokees living in Lystra, and Wendy lived on the family's old land near Buffalo Creek, an area that flash flooded even in weak thunderstorms. She had boarded Confetti with Pat in an attempt to keep the horse safe from the water that seemed certain to rise onto her property.

Before Pat's veterinary practice had ever opened, while he was finishing his Cherokee Nation scholarship at the North Carolina State College of Veterinary Medicine, Wendy had operated a full stable. It had done well. At one point she was boarding more than a dozen horses. One of those horses, though—a gelding—had kicked her twice while she was mucking his stall. One hoof hit Wendy in the lower back, ruining a kidney, and as she fell, the other hoof connected with the section of her neck below the cerebral cortex, breaking her spine like an icicle. She was forced to sell her own horses to cover medical expenses—all except Confetti. He was Wendy's favorite. Horses are people, too, she'd said.

Pat had felt a rush of love for Wendy's doctor when he told Pat that Wendy would walk again. It was an even bigger relief when Wendy was finally able to return home from the hospital, not only because Pat loved his sister, but because he had been caring for her six-year-old son, Graham, while she was gone, and things had slipped out of control. Pat had felt confident that he would always be able to resist certain desires around the boy, but he had been wrong.

It started with his simply placing a finger in Graham's mouth, encouraging the boy to suck. This filled Pat with a heretofore unknown physical excitement. The desire to put his nephew's genitalia inside his own mouth, however, was one that he knew was simply unacceptable. Eventually, though, he did it anyway.

Pat had long ago moved to Mankin Park, one of the nicer neighborhoods in Lystra, and his house was a two-mile walk away from his office to the far end of Tripp Lane. Dead branches fell from scrub pines and landed around him as he rode Confetti along the shoulder of the road. They were out of the floodwater now, but the rain was continuous, the grey continuous. Even the falling branches were just solid pieces of grey, slightly darker pieces of the sky settling into the mud at Confetti's hooves.

When he heard the sound of a car approaching from behind, Pat consciously tried not to look. He knew how ridiculous he must seem, riding a horse bareback on Tripp Lane. The wheels ground to a halt on the wet concrete but he kept his head forward.

Then he heard his name.

It was his sister, Wendy. Her horse trailer was attached to her truck and she was already getting out.

Pat had bought the horse trailer for Wendy two weeks before Graham's thirteenth birthday. By then, Pat's veterinary practice had opened and he was paying all of Wendy's expenses—her dialysis, rent, utilities. She was no longer able to work, due to her injuries, and Pat was glad to help. He lived alone; he didn't need all that money. He remembered the date of the trailer purchase because Wendy had called after Graham's birthday party to say that he had just told her some stories, horrible stories, about Pat doing things to him. Sexual things. Poking, licking his privates. Pat acted shocked but forgiving. He told her that Graham needed to know the consequences of lying, the effect something like that might have on all of their lives. Wendy never even asked Pat if it was true. Pat sounded pained when he suggested that she consider sending Graham to live with his father in Memphis for a while. He pointed out that Wendy had been having a hard time caring for him anyway, in her condition.

Graham eventually had gone to Memphis, where he was now a sophomore in high school. In addition to providing for Wendy, Pat also wrote a monthly check that she sent to Graham.

Pat hadn't spoken to his nephew in over two years. He now had control. He just kept it to photos and videos—a stash of items that he bought from The Matchbox Adult Bookstore on Route 60 and hid in a plastic storage bin in the back of his walk-in closet.

— — —

"Just look at you," Wendy said, stepping towards Pat through the rain. Her black hair was loose, hanging wet and stringy far past her uneven shoulders. Since the accident, her body had been utterly erased of symmetry. Her spine curved out one way near her shoulders, her head permanently angled in the opposite direction.

"The office—" Pat said.

"I know. I heard Elm Street was flooding, so I just drove over. I couldn't even make it to Lee, though. Hey boy, yeah. Hey."

"The truck died," Pat said, sliding off Confetti's wet back. "And this was all I could think to do."

"Your posture looked good," Wendy said, leading the horse to her trailer.

Inside Wendy's truck, water dripped off Pat and puddled in the seat bottom as he shivered, exhausted. Wendy gave him her knit pullover, but it didn't stop the shaking.

"Water's already in the house," she said.

"It'll be alright," Pat said. "I got flood insurance for you on the last policy. It'll be fine. Just stay at my place."

"Where's everything else?" she said.

"At home. The dogs I put upstairs, but the cats I just let loose. I didn't have time to situate everything. And now," he held up his hand, "there's this."

"Pat."

"I fell."

The area around the splinter was filling with fluid and his wrist was already swollen.

"You need to get that out."

"I know."

"We'll get it out," Wendy said.

At Pat's house, a two-story stucco, Wendy put Confetti in the garage as Pat went inside. Cats were everywhere. Some were sleeping, some were hiding. Some of them were still in their carriers, even though the doors stood open. Pat knew that when cats sensed an ominous change in weather, they searched out small places in which to hide. The dogs were barking on the second floor; the lizards were sleeping in three glass aquariums in the kitchen. He didn't know where the rabbit had hidden.

Pat went straight to the bathroom, stripped, and began to run a hot shower. Without electricity, his bathroom was barely manageable, only a dim bit of light coming through a section of glass brick in the wall. Horsehair and mud covered his arms, and he knew he needed to wash his hand before he cut out the splinter. Wendy had told him that she would have ice ready for his hand when he came out. She always fawned over him. Once he began paying her bills, it was all he could do to not have her calling every hour to see if he needed anything. Dry cleaning? Floors waxed? Dinner?

After the shower, his hand throbbed from the heat. The skin was going to need to be cut. In his medicine cabinet Pat kept a small box of Tetracaine samples. Tetracaine was a local anesthetic used for animals. He applied a generous amount to his palm, then took an orange bottle from the shelf and shook out a pill the size of a wasp. He put his head under the tap, and the pill, a Ketaset horse tranquilizer, struggled down his throat. Ketaset was an anesthetic, but in some people elicited a type of rapture. Out of curiosity, Pat had taken one before, but it had only rendered him comatose.

Pat stepped into the living room but stopped when he saw Wendy on the couch. On the table before her sat the plastic storage bin, the one filled with his photos, his unique photos, the ones he special-ordered from the owner of The Matchbox. They were all of boys. Young boys. His most recent ones were of a four-year-old in a hay loft with two grown men, bearded and naked.

"What are you doing with that?" Pat said.

"A cat was crying in your closet," Wendy said. She looked scared, her face almost sideways, its muscles drawn taut and severe.

"That's some crazy stuff, isn't it?" Pat said.

"What?"

"Did you look in there?"

"It was open," Wendy said. "The cat was in there. What is this?"

humans fall into my field

"What is in that box is hard to understand if you're not a scientist."

Wendy looked so confused that her expression was almost one of pain.

"What's in that box is data," Pat said. "You see what I'm saying? It's a medical study. It doesn't mean anything, nothing other than just me looking at some scientific photos."

"But it's sick," Wendy said.

"Oh, I know it is. I know. What's in that box, it shouldn't be seen by anyone who isn't scientific. I hid those photos for a reason."

"But those aren't even animals," Wendy said.

"I'm studying life," Pat said. "All animal forms. Their perversions, the abnormalities. Humans are animals, Wendy. They fall into my field."

"These," Wendy said, pointing to the box, "aren't for studying."

"Well that's what I'm doing, Wendy. I'm studying life, OK? I am just curious about animal activity. I don't want to get into it, really, because I've only just begun this study. But trust me, some experiments you leave in the abstract. Some questions you only ask in the hypothetical."

"What are you talking about?" Wendy said. "What does that mean?"

"It means that these are just photos. What? Wendy, what?"

"So, do you like this? Boys?" Wendy said.

"Jesus!" Pat said. "Do you even understand what I do? You don't even understand half the words I'm using! Hypothetical! See? Abstract! See? Watch this. Empirical data! Jesus. Just trust me, Wendy. I'm doing stuff you can't even understand." He paused, then said, "Oh God. I didn't mean for it to sound like that. Hey."

Wendy looked at him as if he were a stranger.

"What?"

"You did it," Wendy said.

Fear had ambushed all of Pat's operating mechanisms. He could only shake his head. Finally he said, "Did what? These are just paper!"

Wendy shook her head.

"Are you still talking about Graham?" Pat said. "Because you were the one who told me that he had made all that stuff up. Remember?" He sat on the opposite end of the couch. "We've talked about this."

"No. I don't think so," Wendy said.

"I would never do anything to Graham," Pat said. "Come on! Who just led Confetti through a goddamn flood? Who pays your bills? I love you, Wendy. Keykeyu," he said, the Cherokee word for love. "Hey, keykeyu."

Wendy just looked at the carpet.

"You want me to go back over this?" Pat said. "Listen. Kids make up stories, Wendy, especially when they don't have a father. He also, and I don't want to bring this up, but he also probably resented me somehow for paying for everything, you know? He had to become reliant on a new person. Because, and again, I don't want to bring it up, but neither of you could have even stayed in your neighborhood, let alone paid the bills, if I hadn't been able to help. He knew that. And still, Wendy, I love that I am fortunate enough to help you. Keykeyu."

Wendy was silent for a long time as the cats continued to meow throughout the room. One began rubbing against her leg, then Wendy sighed and said, "That doesn't have anything to do with this. Nothing." She looked up at Pat. "Tell me you did it."

But Pat didn't say anything.

"Say it."

Pat slowly shook his head.

humans fall into my field

Then Wendy stood and walked across the dark living room, cats scurrying out of her path. He heard her open the back door, but he knew she had nowhere to go.

Pat thought about what Wendy now knew. There wasn't actual proof. Unconnected photos are not proof. His pulse was racing and he could hear dogs barking upstairs. The rabbit hopped from under the couch and looked at him.

He decided he needed to act like their discussion wasn't that big a deal. He stood, but his balance was off and he wavered a bit. The Ketaset had begun to work. He carried the bin of photos to the coat closet, just to get it out of sight, then walked into the kitchen. He was feeling very strange, very loose. The pain was receding. He looked out the back window and saw Wendy standing in the garage doorway, rubbing Confetti's nose. There was an apple on the counter, and Pat took one of his small, good knives off the knife rack and sliced it in half. His hand was feeling much better and he almost cut the splinter out right then, but decided to wait for the Tetracaine's full effect.

Outside, the air was a solid form of rain, drops replaced by more drops, small rivulets of water forming everywhere in his drive-way.

"Maybe some apple?" Pat said, stepping up behind Wendy. He was already soaked from walking only the fifteen feet between the garage and his house.

Wendy moved into the darkness, silent. Pat couldn't see her face.

"Hey, boy. Yeah," Pat said, as Confetti rubbed his nose against Pat's chest. He held his good hand open and Confetti's soft lips brushed Pat's skin as the horse lifted the apple. "I thought this might make him feel better," Pat said. "What about you? Are you OK?"

Wendy sighed and said, "I don't know."

He could tell she had been crying.

"You want me to get you some apple, too?" Pat said, laughing slightly. He felt nauseated. He hadn't made his sister cry in decades. Wendy didn't answer, and Pat said, "OK. Come inside soon."

He could barely feel the rain now as it landed on his flesh.

Back in the kitchen, he stood at the counter and thought about what he could do to make Wendy feel better. He would cook the venison now thawing in the dead freezer, maybe open that bottle of zinfandel. She loved good wine. He took the venison out and set it on a plate, then looked closely at his palm. He poked it with his finger. He could barely feel the pressure now. He lifted the knife from the counter and tried to focus. He felt funny, light, but steady enough to make a small incision above the splinter. As soon as the blade sliced into his flesh, though, pain shot through his arm. Pus and blood came rushing out of the opening, pressurized by the swelling. He pressed a clean dish towel to his hand and walked to the couch. He felt unsteady and thought he should lie down. As he reclined, a calico jumped onto his chest, purring. Pat closed his eyes, then opened them, and now there was a different cat on his chest—a black cat meowing. Time was condensing. He thought about the number of seconds it took to make one mistake. He had probably spent a total matter of minutes touching Graham. Minutes. Maybe a few hundred seconds. He thought about the grown dogs he had seen humping teddy bears, human legs, puppies. People laughed. A man can make a mistake.

It was growing difficult to keep his eyes open, and he felt himself falling asleep when Wendy came back inside. He heard her moving stuff around in the kitchen, banging and scraping, and when he opened his eyes again, he saw her coming towards him out of the darkness. Her clothes were completely soaked and water dripped from her cocked head. She was moving slowly, carrying the kitchen knife that he had used to cut the apple.

"Oh!" Pat said, the sound stretching much longer than he had intended, eerie and loud and uncontrolled in the silence. "Please. Wendy." He tried to stand and felt himself going sideways.

"Pat. You need to calm down," Wendy said. She was standing over him now. "I'm going to get that splinter out."

Pat tried to stand again slowly, dizzy.

"No. Lie down," Wendy said. "What's wrong with you?" She gently pushed him back down.

"Aghh!" Pat screamed.

"Pat, cool it."

"I have always done what I could to keep you safe," Pat said.

Wendy sat on his chest and grabbed his arm. Pat tried reaching around with the other, but then Wendy said, "Don't move, Pat. Don't! I'm serious."

He froze.

"I have done everything," Pat said, "everything, to show you I loved you. Keykeyu, Wendy. Keykeyu. Keykeyu. Keykeyu."

He couldn't see what she was doing with the knife, but he felt her cutting into his flesh. There was no pain—the Ketaset had finally taken care of that—but still he screamed in terror, silencing all animal noise.

"Shhhhh," Wendy said.

Then she stopped cutting and turned to him. Blood dripped off her hand and onto Pat's chest. She held the splinter aloft, pinched between two fingers. It was a dark, bloody intruder.

the gypsy

Cotton's eyesight was still good, and as he squinted, peering down the narrow basement stairs, the situation slowly became clear. The flashlight beam was reflecting off the surface of water. He should have checked earlier. Always check the basement in a storm, Cotton thought. Always.

He bent to remove his orthopedic shoes, then rolled up his slacks and started slowly down the stairs, the flashlight slicing erratically through the darkness. His scrapbooks, his photo albums—all of his genealogy research was in the basement. He needed to get it out before the water rose that high.

As he descended, he could hear the rain drumming on the roof and now also dripping inside. He had expected Hurricane Hugo to bring enough rain to wet the floor, perhaps. That had happened before, but this? The water was already covering several basement stairs, and as the fleshy sole of Cotton's foot came down on the first submerged step, it slipped out from under him and his body lifted briefly into the darkness.

He awoke with water lapping at his sternum. His back was propped against the bottom two stairs and his legs stretched onto the concrete floor, almost completely submerged in the shallow water. The steps bit at angles into his spine, and his head felt as if large pockets of air needed to be released from it immediately. Worst off was his left leg. Something was horribly wrong with it. Even the slightest movement was unbearable.

The flashlight was now underwater, throwing an undulating series of dim lights onto the concrete wall. The rest of the room was dark and his eyes began to adjust to minuscule rays of daylight shining through chinks in the floorboards above.

He tried to rise, putting his weight on his arms and good leg, but there was a terrifying, paralyzing pain as soon as he began to move.

He had seen this injury before.

From 1955 to 1977, Cotton had been a NASCAR crew chief. The driver for his 1962 team, a young man named Scooter Matthews, had broken his hip in a rollover at Charlotte Motor Speedway. It had been bad enough on a twenty-year-old, but in the years since, Cotton had seen what it had done to friends his own age. A surge of nausea rose as he imagined ivory chunks of hip and femur floating around the marbleized gristle of his thigh. He closed his eyes and exhaled.

From his experience with injuries on the racetrack, Cotton knew not to move an injured body, but his muscles were tense with the chill and beginning to spasm. He tried to remain still as the prospect of the next few months spread itself before him. The wheelchairs, the surgery, the scars, and the painkillers. He didn't know how he was going to afford it, how he would care for Lee.

Lee was Cotton's grandson, the only son of his only daughter, Laura. Laura was autistic and lived in Green Valley Assisted Care off of Highway 220. God only knew how they had let it happen, but Green Valley was also where she'd gotten pregnant. That had been in 1979, the father another autistic boy who lived there. There had been a settlement and quite a bit of brouhaha, including talk of abortion, but this was a grandson, Cotton had thought. He knew there wouldn't be another chance. After spending so many years near bodies hurtling towards metal and asphalt, Cotton had come to believe in a profound sanctity of life. He had pulled so many drivers out of mangled stock cars that the last thing he felt he could do was kill off a grandson before the kid even had a chance.

So Cotton was now a single grandparent with a nine-year-old boy. His wife, Nora, had been dead for three years before Lee was even born, and Cotton knew no other single fathers in Lystra, let alone grandfathers. But he was happy to have Lee. He'd seen what happened to other friends who'd retired and lost wives. There was a general decline, a closing in and surrender, but Cotton felt the urgency of imparting all knowledge to this boy, of staying alive long enough to do so.

He called out, but his voice was weak and Lee wasn't home to hear it anyway. School had been cancelled because of Hugo, and Cotton had agreed to let Lee go down the street to his friend Donnie's house.

The face of his watch was still visible in the dim light and he saw that it was only a few minutes after two o'clock. Lee wouldn't be home until three.

▱ ▱ ▱

Cotton had found that as he aged, the greater his desire was to create a clear picture of his family tree. He began studying genealogy at the library, even ordering a family tree assemblage kit out of the back of *Parade* magazine. When it arrived, though, it was basically just an empty photo album with loose-leaf charts full of blanks that Cotton couldn't fill. He would have called his distant relatives, but there was no one living to call. He organized all the family photos into the album. He had a handful of portraits from Nora's side and a few of himself as a child, but the majority of these photos were of Laura as a girl. There had been a period of parental ignorance—from birth until she was three—that had indeed been bliss. It was during this time, a span when it was not yet clear that Laura had any serious abnormalities, that it seemed Cotton and Nora's new family was off to the perfect start, and they took the photos to prove it. Trips to Myrtle Beach, Tweetsy Railroad,

Grandfather Mountain, Pensacola, and so many racetracks. After the diagnosis, however, the photos stopped being taken. They seemed a willful creation of future painful reminders.

Cotton now prized those photos and wished there had been more. More of Laura, more of Nora. More even of himself.

With Lee, Cotton had documented everything. He thought of this as a practical matter—he simply knew that he wouldn't be around to tell stories of Lee's childhood, so he wanted the photos to be there when he wasn't. He also felt strongly that it was important, regardless of the difficulty, for Lee to have a relationship with his mother. This was why, a few times a month, Cotton drove Lee to Green Valley Assisted Care.

Green Valley was not unlike a nursing home. There were apartments and caregivers and roomfuls of zombified bodies looking up towards the walls of white brick lounges, but Green Valley was assisted care for those who were incapacitated not only by age. The last visit had been warm and sunny. That had been a week earlier, and mid-September was still holding on to August's humidity. Cotton had taken Laura outside and arranged her in a lawn chair. She slumped a bit over the right arm, mesmerized as Lee spun in a slow arc across the lawn, performing a series of karate kicks and tumbles over the short grass. Laura laughed loudly, in snorts and gasps, as Lee jumped and kicked and then fell to the grass and rolled before popping up again. Cotton wondered where Lee had learned this. Did they teach karate in fifth grade now? After finishing his routine, Lee approached Cotton and Laura, and Laura put up her hand for a high five. This was a move she had picked up from one of the male nurses, and it seemed to put Lee very much at ease. Cotton held his hand up, too, and Lee slapped it.

On the car ride home, Lee said that his friend Donnie had taught him the karate, and Cotton explained that there were other sports that were more rewarding. Team sports. Lee said karate was more of a sport than NASCAR. Cotton knew this to not be true. He explained that most people didn't think of NASCAR as a team sport, but that it was. That it's teamwork that creates wins. Cotton knew that he didn't have forever to set these examples, to teach these lessons. Probably only single-digit years.

= = =

By the time the flashlight died, the stairs felt as if they had permanently formed Cotton's spine into a *W*. The pain in his hip had become almost funny, a ludicrous scientific experiment. He couldn't see his wristwatch anymore, but when last he looked, it had been about half till three. The water had risen up to his lower neck now, and although he knew it was rising slowly, he worried that it might eventually reach his face.

He was trying to remove himself from the moment—this was what he had always told his injured drivers to do—but his attention turned to the increasingly unavoidable needs of his bladder. He quit trying to hold things indefinitely and just began to relieve himself right there on the stairs. This was when he finally heard the front door open, and a thrill, an electric jolt, shot through him, making the warm urine shoot out even more rapidly into the cold water.

Footsteps crossed the floor above. The house was small and old, making it easy to follow any movement. The steps creaked loudly inside, were more muffled in the carpeted living room, then pulsed down the hall, pausing at Lee's bedroom, and finally stopped in the vicinity of Cotton's bedroom.

"Hello!" Cotton called. His voice sounded alien, a high and panicked warble. "Hello! Lee?"

He heard the footsteps move tentatively. Two, three steps. Then stop. Nothing. The water continued to drip.

"Hello?" Cotton called. "Hello! Who's there? Lee?" Even to his own ear, his voice sounded pitiful and scary. "Please! Lee? Come here!"

Nothing. No footsteps.

"Could you please help me? Hello?"

Cotton was scared and cold, the pain dangerously close to overwhelming him. He felt it like a stain seeping into his otherwise clear thoughts.

The footsteps started up again. They crossed back towards the front hall. Now they were in the kitchen. Now they stopped. Again they were coming closer. Cotton looked up the stairs, towards the open door, and a dark form slid into view, backlit against the dim light. It was the silhouette of a large man holding a plastic trash bag.

"Hello?" Cotton said.

The man said nothing. He just stood there.

Cotton's nausea returned and this time he actually vomited. Barely a mouthful of liquid shot onto the stairs.

"Please help me."

The man continued to stand in silence.

"You can take whatever you want," Cotton said. "There is a very nice clock right beside you on the counter. You can take that. Please."

Cotton could make out nothing other than the man's silhouette. It was too much to hold his head at the angle required to look at him, though, and he finally just lay in the tiny pool of vomit.

This was when the man finally spoke.

"[French.]"

Cotton didn't speak French but he knew what it sounded like. The man had clearly just said something to him in French.

"I'm sorry? Hello?"

"[French.]"

"I'm sorry, but I can't understand you."

"[French.]"

"I cannot understand you. Do. You. Speak. English?"

"No."

"I've fallen and I think my hip is broken. Do you understand?"

"[French.]"

"Do you understand 'emergency'?"

The man set down his bag, took five steps down to where Cotton lay, and bent over. He was still backlit and Cotton could not make out his face. He grabbed Cotton underneath each shoulder and lifted him from the stairs. The pain was overwhelming. Lights flashed before his eyes and he screamed out in a high, cracking yelp. The man then set Cotton on the dry stairs and started back into the kitchen. Cotton moaned and gasped for air as his bones readjusted to new angles.

From above, the refrigerator door opened and closed. A few cabinets banged open and shut. The man was taking his time now. As he tried to catch his breath, Cotton listened to the man leave the house and then return. This happened three times. Because the footsteps soon led back to his bedroom, Cotton now guessed that the man had found Nora's jewelry, which he kept, along with his cuff links and collar stays, in a wooden box on his dresser. Her engagement ring had belonged to his grandmother and was the only real heirloom he owned. It had become more precious to Cotton as his interest in genealogy had grown, but he found it less important right now than his desire to have this man out of the house before Lee returned.

Cotton heard the front door open again. This, he hoped, meant that the man was gone for good, but then suddenly the man appeared again at the top of the stairs and stepped into the basement. He silently shut the door, making the small beams of light creeping through the floor stand out even more against the now deeper darkness.

"Shhhhhhhh," the man said, crouching on the steps above Cotton. "[French.]"

Cotton listened. There was someone else in the house.

"Granpy!" came from upstairs. Little footsteps scurried across the floorboards, finally stopping in the living room.

The man smelled like a wet dog. The water was still dripping into the basement, and on top of that sound Cotton could hear the rain, the man breathing, and his own teeth chattering.

Lee's little footsteps spread slowly throughout the house, stopping in other rooms, opening closets, circling.

"Grandpa? Hello?"

"Shhhhhh," the man said again.

Cotton didn't even think about calling out. This was the safe thing. Silence. Lee's little footsteps entered the kitchen. Leave, Cotton thought, just leave. He heard the pantry door open. Surely Lee was noticing items missing. Please don't look down here, Cotton thought. Just go back to Donnie's house. Go.

Then the basement door opened and Lee's silhouette appeared in the rectangle of dim light.

"Grandpa?"

"[French!]" the man said, standing up.

"Lee," Cotton said. "It's OK."

"[French! French! French!]" the man yelled, now stepping up the stairs towards Lee.

Lee crouched slightly and then methodically carved his hands into the air, as if they were attached to a low, slow gear.

"Lee," Cotton said.

"I don't know you," Lee said, then karate-chopped the man in the face.

The man's head whipped to the side and Lee's little footsteps rushed across the floor and the front door shut.

Cotton had taught Lee emergency procedure many, many times. Even if he didn't remember what to do—which was probable, Cotton thought—he would at least run to Donnie's house and tell his parents. They were teachers. They were at home today. They would know what to do.

The man never looked at Cotton again. He walked up the stairs and then his footsteps slowly crossed the house. He was obviously not chasing after Lee, and finally Cotton heard the front door squeak and thud.

The sirens were clear for a long time before they finally stopped in the street. There was a cavalcade of boots. Flashlights, their multiple beams crossing, exploded into the basement with so many voices at once. Cotton was strapped to a yellow gurney and glided into the living room on the shoulders of young men. The television, the new answering machine, Lee's Intelevision, he couldn't tell what else. They were gone.

"You saw the man?" a voice said.

"Yes," Cotton said. He couldn't see who was speaking.

They were now going through the front door. Someone held an umbrella above him, trying to keep the rain off, but it wasn't working well, and Cotton's face was getting rained on.

"And he attacked you?"

"No, no. I slipped."

"During the confrontation?"

"The . . . ?"

"He said there was a confrontation."

"Who?"

"Your son."

"No. I had already fallen."

Lee stood at the curb with Donnie's parents, Janet and Dave Organtip, thin and windblown in their noisy bright rain jackets. Lee looked terrified and was holding Janet's boney hand.

Dave called out, "We've got Lee, Cotton. We'll see you at the hospital. Hang in there!"

The gurney crunched against the edge of the ambulance. Its collapsible legs folded and more rain fell on Cotton's face before he was inside.

"OK. Your son—" the floating voice said.

"Grandson."

"I'm sorry. It's just, we want to get this as quick as we can. I'm sorry. But your son, grandson, said that he attacked the man."

"Lee did karate."

"Karate?"

"Lee calls them karate chops."

"Your son struck the gypsy?"

"Gypsy?" Cotton said.

He had heard about them all his life. People in North Carolina blamed almost every burglary on them. They were the ones who came into town and broke into your house, usually during the day. They would send their children to the front door to ask where their lost dog was while the parents snuck in the back. They would come in your house when you went to the grocery store, even while you were gardening. They posted lookouts at the end of the block to blow whistles if someone was coming. They stole babies. Picked your tomatoes. Used your swimming pool. Cotton had friends who claimed to have seen them. His own parents said they had, many times. They were dark, people said. But Cotton had never thought they were real.

"They've been all over today," the man said. "All over the place. So let me get this straight. Your son struck the gypsy?"

"Grandson. He calls them karate chops."

the gypsy

"Jesus Christ. You hear that? A nine-year-old attacked the gypsy."

Cotton closed his eyes as the vehicle began to roll. The lights from the ambulance were comforting, seeping red through Cotton's eyelids. These were the lights of an emergency vehicle, a machine whose engine he knew inside out, a system of safety and communication he understood and had used countless times.

At Wesley Long, Cotton was attached to a morphine drip and propped on an adjustable mattress that smelled like plastic. The hospital had power running off of a generator. Outside, Cotton could see the rain still falling and that the streetlights were dark. He wondered if the water in his basement was still rising.

Lee stood near Cotton's right shoulder. Dry tufts of blond hair stood up against darker wet spots, clearly the effect of someone having towel dried his hair, and he was wearing clothes that Cotton did not recognize.

"Was he really a gypsy?" Lee asked.

"He was an intruder."

"He took my Intelevision."

"Mmm."

"Are we going to get a new TV?"

"Mmm."

"Mrs. Organtip said that I am a vigilante. That's like The Punisher."

Lee was deep into a comic-book stage.

"A lot of people are real excited right now," Cotton said, "but I'm going to tell you that what you did was not smart. You cannot act like that." Cotton let that sink in. "When you're dealing with people like that, you just let the man have what he wants. You hear me?"

"Yes, sir."

If there were a world where Cotton was not the only one raising Lee, if there were others to set the rules and examples, he might admit that what Lee had done was brave. Cotton had this in him. He had always admired drivers who risked safety successfully in service of a win. These people had networks of rules, systems of social examples that they could break and return to knowingly. Lee, though, had only Cotton.

"I want you to know that I am glad you are OK. You did well enough by calling emergency."

"Yes, sir."

"That was a job well done. Now, why don't you go get the Organtips. I want to talk to them."

Lee left the room and Cotton continued to look out the window at the rain and the fading light.

There's a saying in NASCAR that if a crew ain't cheating, it ain't trying. Cotton knew it was true, that sometimes you had to work outside of the rules, even lie to get things done for your teammates. He didn't know how else he might do it, but he thought he might have to fib a little to get the Organtips to take Lee in until he got out of the hospital. He would need to make it seem like the injury wasn't serious, that he'd be out of there right away. In truth, he had no idea how long it would take. The orthopedic surgeon had yet to come in.

The Organtips rustled into the room behind Lee. Both coached high school track and were wiry and athletic, yet something about their physiques seemed unhealthy to Cotton. They were so veiny. Especially in this fluorescent light, it was like they both had some excess vein structure that was forcing its way up and out of the skin. Lee stood at the window, his back to the adults, and Cotton could tell from the way he was fidgeting that he was ready to leave.

"Cotton," Janet said.

the gypsy

"How are you?" Dan said.

"Fine, fine. These things happen all the time. I want to thank you so much for bringing Lee here."

"Not at all."

Cotton had barely ever spoken to them before, usually only waving when he drove by, or giving them the quick OK to take Lee on different outings with Donnie. The boys never played at Cotton's house.

"They said it'll be a pretty quick procedure," Cotton said. "In and out, really. I hate to ask you this, but I'm worried about my basement. I don't know if you know someone who might could—"

"Already done it," said Dan. "Took a look right before we came. The water's still rising. Storm drains filled up with leaves and stuff pretty early on this morning, and the whole system is screwy. There must be a cracked main drain somewhere, but you're not the only one. The whole street is filling up. I spoke to the work crew out there now, and they said that it looked like things would be slowing down pretty soon, mostly because of the rain tapering off."

"Oh boy. Oh boy," Cotton said. He had never assumed that Dan would just take a look without being asked. "I have some books down there. Photos."

"It's no problem. I'll get them when we go back."

"And," Janet said, "we would love to have Lee for as long as you're here."

She beat him to the question. How long had it been since he'd had someone do him a favor? How long had it been since he had really even interacted with a neighbor, or anyone other than Lee? He felt embarrassed for having thought he might need to trick these people.

"I . . ." Cotton said. "That would be wonderful. Thank you."

"It's our pleasure. The little hero."

"Oh, this karate. It's got to stop," Cotton said.

It occurred to him that Lee had so many friends. He had Donnie, and schoolmates, and now even their parents. Cotton's friends were gone. Little Mike Tankersly was still living in Reidsville—he had been on Cotton's pit crew for thirteen years—and Laura was at Green Valley, but there was no one in Lystra, really, no one he could call a friend.

"Lee, does that sound alright?"

Lee turned from the window.

"Yeah."

He sounded excited.

"Good," Cotton said. "I'll be out of here and like new before you know it. This hip, it's plain smashed. But they're going to switch it out. It's like putting in a new carburetor these days. These guys, they just switch them out."

"Yes, sir." Lee said. He was barely paying attention.

"So don't you worry about me."

"Yes, sir."

"Just forget about it. Tell me what you did today."

Lee started speaking quickly. It was his I-want-to-go tone. "Um. We found this trampoline and then later Jessica and Madeline and Will and Henry came over and we played light as a feather stiff as a board."

"Whoa. Slow down." Cotton had no idea who these people were. "Tell me about this game." He didn't want Lee to leave quite yet.

"It's when, like I lay down, and then everyone puts two fingers underneath me, and then they all chant, 'Light as a feather, stiff as a board,' and then they can pick you up like it's nothing. Like I was a feather. It's awesome."

"I'll be dog," Cotton said.

"Yes, sir."

Cotton envisioned a group of children carrying Lee around a

dark room with their fingertips. He wondered if they'd been doing this while he lay on the stairs.

"I'll call as soon as I have any sort of information," Cotton said. "If you can just write down your number, I—"

Janet wrote a string of numbers on a hospital menu, her jacket making so much noise that Cotton could barely hear the rain.

"Lee. Lee, where are you? Lee. Look at me. Manners do matter."

"Yes, sir."

"OK. Dan, Janet."

"There's a breath in and a breath out. That's all that we have," Dan said, swishing near the bed. "So breathe." He placed his veiny hand on Cotton's shoulder. This was surely some coaching maxim Dan used with the track team, and it was a bit too much for Cotton. It embarrassed him, though he remembered similar things that he'd said to his own drivers. What was it that he had said?

"Thank you."

Lee was in the hallway now, looking back in towards Cotton while holding Janet's hand. Dan swished out, the door silently swinging shut behind him, and through its small window, a square of wired glass, Cotton watched them pass.

The rain seemed louder in their absence, clicking like fingernails against the exterior windowpane. If it didn't stop soon, Cotton thought, it was going to rise into his house. It would well up into his kitchen, sweep across the linoleum, and run through his living room, washing down the hall and into their bedrooms. The beds would be ruined and the carpets would have to be removed. His photo albums might already be swelling up. Laura's baby pictures could, at that very moment, be floating across the surface of the floodwater.

He tried to think of how much it was all going to cost. The repairs. The surgery.

He owned some cars. There were three that he kept in storage, in Little Mike's garage. He never even worked on them anymore. He could sell those, he thought. That might cover the surgery. And if the water damage was only in the basement, maybe they wouldn't have to do any repair. Four thousand. Three. There would be other bills, too, though. Constants. Laura's bills. Telephone. Gas. He closed his eyes and tried to calm down. In the only building with electricity in downtown Lystra, Cotton added up how much would be left over.

floodmarkers

⊘　⊘　⊘　⊘　⊘　⊘　⊘　⊘　⊘

Fletcher stood at the edge of the floodwater in her front yard as her older brother Mike blew air into the mouth of her best friend Grier. Grier lay on her back, wearing only her underwear. Water lapped gently over her feet. Mike was blowing too many long breaths into her, though, and with her head at the wrong angle like that—chin tucked against the sternum—Fletcher knew that the air wouldn't reach Grier's lungs.

"Stop," she said.

Mike's lips parted from Grier's as he turned to look at Fletcher. His embarrassing six-inch mohawk—a construction he maintained with the annoying and perpetual practice of microwaving a small bowl of cherry Jell-O every morning and then rubbing the liquefied gelatin into his hair—was now drooping in the rain. Jell-O ran in red streaks down his face.

Fletcher knew CPR from lifeguarding at the Lystra Country Club but had only ever practiced resuscitation on CPR Annie, a mannequin torso with latex lips that smelled like balloons.

"You're not doing it right," Fletcher said.

"Well, help!"

Fletcher looked at the cold water, its surface pocked by countless raindrops. She wasn't supposed to be out in this.

"Come on!" Mike said.

He looked so hopeful. So needful of Fletcher. It was a look he had never given her before. She fell to her knees in the shallow water and pushed his hands away.

Earlier that morning, before sunrise, before Hurricane Hugo had knocked the electricity out, before the water had risen out of Mankin Park and spread low and stealthy across the neighborhood, Fletcher had seen Grier in bed with her brother. It was the first time she'd found them together naked, but it wasn't a complete surprise. Only weeks earlier Fletcher had discovered them together singing "Sit Down You're Rocking the Boat" in the kitchen. They had their clothes on then and were clearly only practicing for *Guys and Dolls*, but Fletcher could see what was happening. She'd said nothing, only watched unseen from the hallway as they sang "sit down sit down sit down."

Grier smelled like frozen sandwich meat, but her mouth was still warm against Fletcher's lips. With each chest compression, vomit coursed out of Grier's mouth.

"Keep doing that," Mike said.

But Fletcher knew it wasn't Grier who was breathing. This was only her brother's breath being forced out of an inflated stomach.

Throughout elementary school, even most of middle school, Fletcher and Grier had been inseparable. It was an easy, almost inevitable pairing, Grier the wacky, outgoing girl, mousy and underdeveloped; Fletcher the quieter one, beautiful and popular but reliant on Grier for a certain social spark. In the past year, though, Grier had started listening to strange music, wearing vintage dresses, watching old movies—movies with *no talking*. They had moved apart in imperceptible steps, their friendship becoming a compound of memories.

The last real time they'd spent together was when they'd driven Grier's Dodge Diplomat to Myrtle Beach over spring break. Before they reached the beach, Grier stopped at Crazy Barrett's Fireworks.

Crazy Barrett's was famous for having a fireworks testing area—an enclosed Plexiglas room with a concrete floor where you could light one of any firework you wanted.

They gathered as many roman candles, thunder bombs, Saturn batteries, and whistling busters as they could afford—enough fireworks to fill the bottom of a shopping cart—and Grier took them into the testing room. Fletcher watched from the other side of the scarred Plexi as Grier sent colored sparks shooting in arcs across the space. She looked electric in that smoky cell, like it was her exploding, not a cardboard cylinder that read GUCCI MINESHELL MAYHEM. That was three months before Fletcher got sick, but even then it was clear that Grier was more alive.

The taste of Grier's vomit was not as bad as Fletcher had expected. Her own sickness had rendered the body's various productions innocuous, just annoying byproducts of an unreliable factory. After three more breaths, Fletcher put her hands between Grier's small breasts and forced a small stream of water out of her mouth with each compression. Then something popped, loud and solid under Fletcher's palms.

"What's that?" Mike said.

Fletcher knew that it was normal for ribs to break during compressions, but she didn't say anything, she just continued to pump.

"Hey!" Mike yelled towards the closest houses. "Help!"

Grier's flesh seemed pristine, preserved, as if she had just emerged from a melting block of ice.

"Is she dead?" Mike said.

"I don't know," Fletcher said.

"She's dead?"

"I don't know."

"You sure?"

"I don't know!"
"Fuck!"
Mike lay his ear against Grier's chest.

When they were young, Fletcher and Mike had been close. For
almost the whole summer after their parents divorced, when
Fletcher was nine and Mike twelve, she slept on the floor of his
bedroom in a sleeping bag. At times, she would even climb onto his
bed and he would stay up with her, talking. Now he was eighteen
and barely spoke to her. She didn't understand his transformation,
why he shut her out and put Jell-O in his hair and drove a monster
truck.

"I don't hear anything," Mike said.
Fletcher resumed her pumping and another rib popped. Her
sickness had given her a perspective on bodily damage. A rib would
heal, a head of hair would grow back. Previously, the closest she'd
ever come to this calm assurance was during the hundred-yard
backstroke, pushing herself through the chlorine with the sensation of molecular fire spreading through her limbs. There was an
end, she would think, gazing at the metal girders arced across the
green gym roof, water splashing across her view. She tried to think
the same thing about the nausea that accompanied her chemotherapy. She knew this logic had worked for swimming. She held six
North Carolina records. Grier's broken ribs were the burn on the
way to the win, Fletcher thought. She was preparing to awaken.
Mike was crying. He wiped at his nose, then got up and started
to run towards Evelyn Graham's house.

Fletcher had never told Grier that she saw her singing with Mike. It
would have been so important before. She wondered if she didn't

care now because of the drugs. She took so many drugs. The only time she ever felt better was when she took her buffet of pills. She longed for the hour of medication.

Fletcher's head was cold. She had read that some huge percentage of your body heat can escape from your scalp, and since her hair had fallen out, she constantly wore a red knit cap. She'd left it inside, though, and now her scalp was exposed. Chemotherapy can shut down your immune system. She was actively thinking about the fact that she was thinking about that, and not Grier. She thought, I wonder if I'm calm because of the drugs. But she didn't think that was it. She put her lips back on Grier's, the vomit now washed away by the rain. The sound of Mike pounding on Mrs. Graham's door carried across the street, and then Fletcher heard them talking. She was still thinking about how she wasn't thinking about Grier. She wasn't drugged, or at least that wasn't the explanation. She was simply calm because she knew Grier was getting ready to cough.

When Fletcher had walked in on Grier and Mike that morning, the only thing she could think about was how thirsty she was. It was like her insides had cracked and withered. The dim glow from the hall nightlight lit the room just enough that she could see them in the bed together and it hadn't mattered at all. All she wanted was something to make her feel better. When she asked Mike for help, Grier tried to hide under the sheets. Fletcher hadn't even laughed, hadn't done anything except ask for a glass of water. She didn't think she would throw up before it came, but she did. Sometimes she was so betrayed by her body, so surprised by its output.

What Mike thought Mrs. Graham was going to do was beyond Fletcher. The phone lines were down and the electricity was out.

No one knew CPR better than Fletcher did. This was as good as the situation could get.

"She's going to the hospital!" Mike said, rushing back to her.

Fletcher didn't even respond. She couldn't waste the energy. She put her mouth back on Grier's, pushed three breaths into her small torso, then pumped her broken ribs. Any second now.

Fletcher's mother and Grier's mother had both driven to the beach the day before to board up their condo. If that house had flooded or the walls had collapsed with those two single women inside, Fletcher thought, the kids would all have to move away, spread out to the homes of fathers. It seemed impossible. This park was Fletcher's favorite thing in the world. She didn't take it for granted. She was keenly aware that right across the street from her bedroom was a plot of land that could not be improved upon. Her favorite spot was Mo's rock, an exposed area of stone by the creek bed where her old dog Mo used to love to lap from the water. She was also mystified by the floodmarkers on the bridge, red lines painted with the high-water marks for floods of years past. She never knew who had painted them. They seemed like some prehistoric markings, emerging from the bridge itself. For the first time ever, the bridge was now completely underwater. When it reemerged Fletcher wanted to paint a new floodmarker on the top. It would say OVER THE TOP 1989. She told herself, You need to do it. You really need to do it. Don't chicken out. She felt like she always chickened out. She was going to do it.

Fletcher could feel the broken ribs shifting and was aware of the possibility that one might tear into a lung. She moved higher on Grier's chest, trying to avoid sharp edges.

Mike had stopped talking and was just breathing wet air through his mouth. Mrs. Graham was slowly backing out of her driveway, into the shallow water standing in the street. Fletcher pumped the lower chest of Grier and knew that she was going to breathe. She simply knew it. This was not hope.

Mrs. Graham rolled through the water so slowly that Fletcher was embarrassed for her.

Then Grier coughed.

Fletcher's house had always been the gathering point. They had the beanbags, the tape player in the kitchen. The moments of friendship and the stretches of long silence together had mostly occurred within those walls, so it made sense that Mike carried Grier there and not to her own house. Fletcher ran behind while Grier moaned over Mike's shoulder and continued to leak water from her lungs.

Inside Grier cried and drooled and vomited more water, a seemingly endless amount contained inside her. She said she'd wanted to swim in the park. It was as dumb as Fletcher had thought. Grier said she thought it would have been fun, that she was so stupid. "I'm so stupid," she said. "I'm so stupid." But the idea was enviable, Fletcher thought. Brave. Who else would think that, who else would identify the chance to swim across Mankin Park and then try to take it? It was exactly the type of thing Grier always did and Fletcher never did. Mike carried Grier into the bathroom and began running water into the tub. Fletcher lingered in the kitchen. She wasn't afraid of seeing Grier naked. She'd seen that enough times. She just didn't want to be in there with Mike, watching.

From the front door she watched the water gently wash through the grass in her yard, a daily view rendered suddenly exotic. The curve of the flowerbed was now the bank of a pond. In the middle of the yard the oak tree that she'd almost never noticed before now seemed austere and grand, rising out of the water. A bright red shirt floated by, a brushstroke through the space that had so recently been only a front yard. The neighborhood. There was an alternate view to it all, something other than night and day. It made Fletcher feel alive, in tune with her senses. She wasn't dying. She was a lifesaver. She was a swimmer.

She opened the storm door and walked into the water, the shock of the chill dulled with her legs still wet. She crossed the street, the water reaching up to her calves now, and then into the park, until the water touched her waist. Then she dove in.

Underwater she opened her eyes.

The geography of the park was barely visible as she stroked into the water, but soon Mo's rock appeared below her, the footpath stretching away into the murky depths. She dropped deeper and floated just above the footpath, like a ghost visiting the landmarks of her life, then drifted over the grass and past a small bed of ferns swaying in the water. She felt endangered and rash, flush with the risk of life. She rolled over and the surface of the floodwater appeared grey in the storm light above, shifting and shattered and low. She was in complete control, circling her hands to keep herself in position. Small branches and bits of vegetation floated gently by, yet there was barely any current, just a random spilling of the banks. Soon her lungs began to burn and she reluctantly started to rise. The hour of medication and pillows neared as she floated upwards, and when her nose surfaced at the same time as her toes, rain pounded her emerging flesh like a thousand tapping fingers insisting she awaken.

NIGHT

What you see around me right now is Mankin Park, near downtown Lystra. I am standing on a bridge that has for years served as a marker for floodcrests, where locals paint lines to mark how high the water in the small creek below me rises. As you can see, however, there is nothing left to mark at this hour. If Henry can show you, swing out a little bit. There. The neighbors here are lucky that the water has stopped before it made it into anyone's living room.

Rain has tapered off for the most part, but Hugo still wreaked havoc throughout this historic day. We are going to see clearing skies tonight, with temperatures holding in the low sixties. Water levels here, obviously high, and flash flood warnings remain in effect. For an update on the path of Hugo, let's go to Rob in the studio.

Rob?

frog gigging

⊖   ⊖   ⊖   ⊖   ⊖   ⊖   ⊖   ⊖   ⊖

This was Matthew's crowded lawn, his darkened house, and Nigel could see him now, standing before a half circle of women more than twice his age, holding aloft a martini into which he had placed a piece of dry ice. The glass issued forth a constant flow of steam that tumbled down his forearm as the women laughed hysterically. Nigel had seen Matthew do this countless times before, but for this crowd it was clearly a first.

The only light on the lawn came soft and wavering from seven flaming tiki torches speared into the wet ground. The electricity had been out since that morning, when Hurricane Hugo had blown inland and thrown the edge of itself over Lystra, ruining plans for the wedding Nigel had returned for. It was Matthew's stepsister, Rebecca, who had been married that afternoon in a makeshift ceremony inside Matthew's living room. The rain had now stopped, though, and the neighborhood was celebrating in the tiki light.

"And introducing . . . Nigel Felts!" Matthew announced as Nigel approached.

The women turned away from Matthew's bubbling martini, their faces all war masks of extreme makeup. They wore clothes covered in aggressively sized floral prints. One lady's blouse featured giant lobsters floating across her sagging chest. Various perfumes mixed in a toxic concoction of flowers and musk.

"Nigel," one of the women said, holding out the collar of her lobster blouse. "Did you make this one?"

"Let's see," Nigel said, his nose almost touching her neck. "No. Not ours."

"What about this?" asked another, holding out her collar.

It seemed to Nigel that his trips home were a single, continuous variation of this conversation. He worked in Atlanta as a product manager for a company called American Label. They made 14 percent of the fabric labels in the United States and had contracts with the military, Wrangler's, OshKosh, Fruit of the Loom . . . the list went on. Nigel had been there for six years.

"Clearly you know the Hayes sisters," Matthew said. "And their guest, Mrs. Vanstory?"

Nigel looked at Mrs. Vanstory. He did know her. He had once had such a crush on her daughter that his notebooks from eighth grade read like he had studied nothing but Lily Vanstory. Most boys had found Lily's flat chest and wide, toothy mouth unappealing. Not so for Nigel. He had felt that his appreciation for her revealed a refined taste. The last time Nigel had seen either Mrs. Vanstory or her daughter was during high school. Mrs. Vanstory's face still looked like her daughter's—equine, freckled, and intimidating.

"Nigel. It is so nice to see you," she said. "You were in Lily's class."

"How is she?"

"Good. She's living in Raleigh still. Married Reggie Edwards." Nigel had no idea who this was. "They have a one-year-old. My little sweetie, Ellis."

"Great," Nigel said, looking to Matthew, ready for him to reclaim this conversation. But Matthew was fully absorbed with a perky young woman in pigtails who was rapidly drinking champagne out of a glass shaped like a cowboy boot. The young woman kept laughing and placing her hand on Matthew's chest. She was not Matthew's wife.

"So, Lily's a mom?" Nigel said. "Geez. I remember when we were fifteen and almost killed you."

"When was that?" Mrs. Vanstory said. He was embarrassed that she didn't seem to recall. "When Lily stepped in front of your car?"

"You mean him?" she said, pointing towards Matthew.

"That was me."

"What happened?" said the lobster woman.

"I was driving home one afternoon and saw Lily kissing him at the curb," Mrs. Vanstory said. "Good God. Remember? I swerved into Welborne Ray's oak tree."

"I remember that," Lobsters said. "Killed your old Lincoln."

Nigel thought it had been a Mercedes.

"He even called the police. Welborne did. God." Mrs. Vanstory shook her head as if to erase the memory. "But I could have sworn it was him."

"We do look alike," Nigel said.

Both he and Matthew had thinning blond hair, which lay limply atop their heads like a skull cap, and for years they had both worn dark, thick moustaches. They were not abnormally thin, but because of their similar height, they shared a certain stretched-out quality. Many people thought they were brothers. They were not. They had known each other since the fifth grade, and even though Nigel had not lived in Lystra for years, he still considered Matthew his closest friend.

"Getting old, I guess," she said. "What are you up to now?"

"Labels."

Vaguely, Nigel explained his life in Atlanta. He checked the labels of the other Hayes sisters, but found himself thinking of nothing but that afternoon with Lily. He remembered how the whites of her eyes had turned red from the swimming pool. He remembered the freckles that had appeared on her forehead, as he marveled at the changes that occurred after only a few hours of sunlight. He remembered how she had leaned towards him first, how they had kissed, and how she had said, "What a great summer day" just before stepping back into the road. A piano lesson had been going on somewhere, the notes floating elegant across the lawn. It was still vivid—the freckles, the chlorine, the piano scales, and the thrill. After the car swerved away from Lily and hit the tree, though, the fingers on those keys stopped. He remembered that, too—the silence after the impact.

Nigel found Matthew alone in the garage, unloading two card-board boxes of roman candles into metal buckets. He was working by the beam of a flashlight that he held between his teeth.

"Hold this," Matthew mumbled.

Nigel took the flashlight from Matthew's mouth and wiped the saliva onto his pants.

"So who's Pocahontas?" Nigel said.

"Pocahontas?"

"That girl. Pigtails."

"She works with me."

"Works with you," Nigel said, training the flashlight beam onto a box that promised nine fireballs a candle.

"What?" Matthew said, standing up, an armful of roman candles held to his chest. The flashlight illuminated concentric ovals of dusty concrete at Matthew's feet. Nigel noticed they were wearing the same shoes. He had made those labels.

"I'm not going to lie to you, man," Matthew said.

"I hear you," Nigel said, but he didn't want to hear any more. He didn't have much advice to give. He had dated only one girl during his time in Atlanta: Kylie Crooke, a thin Kansan who had broken up with him after being diagnosed with rheumatoid arthritis. "It isn't you," she'd said, "it's the bones." But Nigel felt pretty sure it had been him.

"Tell me what the perfume squad cornered you about. I saw you checking labels," Matthew said, resuming his fireworks transfer.

"Mrs. Vanstory just told the story about me kissing Lily, you know? When she drove into the tree?"

"About you kissing Lily?" Matthew said. "That was me."

"What?"

"I told you that story a million times. I kissed her and then her mom drove into a tree. In 1979. Why are we even talking about this?"

"Because that was me!"

"Look, I have a Polaroid. It's from that day. Me and her. Not you," Matthew said.

Nigel raised the flashlight beam to Matthew's face. For a moment, before Matthew raised his hands to block the beam, Nigel could see that he was smiling, almost ready to laugh.

Nigel walked out of the garage and into the kitchen, where Matthew's wife, Elena, was smoking at a table with Mrs. Hampton, Matthew's mother. Two gas lamps lit the room, making Elena's jewelry sparkle softly in the lamplight. It seemed she wore gold everywhere, on her neck and ears, in her hair. Elena was from Salamanca, Spain, and as far as Nigel knew, she was the only person living in Lystra who had been born on another continent. After knowing her for years, though, he still felt the need to be formal around her.

"Deviled egg?" Mrs. Hampton said, lifting one off an oval platter.

"No. Thanks," Nigel said. "Elena, do you . . . I'm sorry. Hi, how are you?"

"Fine, Nigel. How are you?" Elena said. Her accent was very heavy.

"Good. You look great." Her clothes were exotic, label makers unknown. "Do you know where Matthew's old photos are?"

As Elena told him, a plume of smoke tumbled out of her mouth and Nigel noticed that even the brown cigarette she was smoking had bands of gold foil sparkling on its filter.

The guest room had a bookshelf filled almost exclusively with photo albums. Nigel scanned their spines by the light of a candle. Twenty, thirty, they took up three shelves. Only one of the albums belonged to Matthew, though. It was an old plastic binder that he had kept since Nigel could remember. The rest were Elena's. Her family, her childhood in Spain.

Nigel paged through Matthew's album. He found himself in almost every photo. There was one of them dressed as women for a sixth-grade play, a shot of them at the awards ceremony for the middle school tennis tournament, where they had been the only entrants and Matthew had won. Birthday parties. Skateboarding at the spillway. And then, in the back, next to a photo of Matthew and Nigel at Myrtle Beach, he found the Polaroid. The flat, washed-out colors made both the grass and the sky different shades of the same grey. Lily was wearing exactly what he remembered her wearing, the Umbros over her swimsuit, the Wild Dunes T-shirt. They were in the same position he remembered, and she was laughing just like she had. And Nigel wasn't in the photo. It was Matthew.

frog gigging

Near the porch, two teenagers dressed in black jeans and tuxedo shirts mixed drinks on a card table. Nigel didn't know how Matthew had pulled this all together. His stepsister was supposed to have been married at the band shell in Mankin Park that afternoon, but after the storm had rendered any outdoor event impossible, they had moved all wedding events inside Matthew's house. They'd arranged everything in a matter of hours, even with the phone lines down. Now that the rain had stopped, people were outside and in, tracking mud everywhere.

Nigel was waiting for a drink from one of the bartenders when he heard someone say, "Hello."

"Hello?" Nigel said to the bartender.

The teenager raised his acne-scarred face from a bottle of whiskey and said, "Huh?"

"Hello," he heard again. It was Elena's voice, accented and soft from behind him.

He turned around. She was smoking another brown-and-gold cigarette and held a trident-shaped metal spear with a green plastic handle.

"What's with that?"

"Matthew says it is for frogs. Could I have a chardonnay, please?" The teen poured wine to the brim of a glass. "He promised that he'd take me."

"Where?" Nigel said.

She held up the spear.

"Now?"

Matthew was tossing someone's baby into the air on the other side of the lawn. The young mother laughed and pointed. Pocahontas stood at his side, clapping her hands in joy.

"You know how?" Elena said.

Nigel had never gigged frogs in his life, but he said, "Yeah. I'll show you."

They entered the woods at the edge of the lawn, near where Nigel knew a creek ran. He had the faint idea that you were supposed to use a spotlight to find the frogs, or to attract them. He'd also never heard of gigging frogs in a creek. They could hear the croaking, though, and just kept walking towards the shifting sounds along the creek bed. Nigel had a mini-flashlight on his keychain that he shone weakly on the water. The creek had risen out of its banks and ran messy and wide through the scrub pines. As they walked, ice tinkled in Nigel's glass. From time to time he glimpsed a tiki lamp shining through the branches.

Elena squealed a lot and kept grabbing Nigel's elbow. As they made their way deeper into the woods, she poked him in the leg with the gig twice. After lunging for only one frog after several minutes, she stopped Nigel and took a large sip of his whiskey. Something splashed into the creek and Elena gasped, then grabbed Nigel around the waist. She pressed her face into his neck and laughed.

Nigel stopped walking and held her. He hadn't done this since Kylie had left him for her bones.

"Ay yay yay," she said. "Where are the frogs?"

"I don't think we're going to catch a frog."

Nigel could tell she was looking at him from the angle of her neck, but he kept his eyes averted, watching the side of her gold necklace glitter in the faint light.

"Matthew can be such an asshole," she said.

Nigel just kept watching her necklace.

"I know what he's doing," Elena said. "He's fucking those sluts."

Nigel had never had a discussion like this with Elena.

"I live here, with him," she said. "You know? I give up all that. I miss my family. I miss . . . I miss Matthew. I miss him when he is fucking these sluts."

Nigel finally let his eyes meet hers. They were full of tears and the only thing that seemed right was to kiss her. Her mouth tasted horrible, like burnt garlic and cigarettes, but he let the kiss linger and so did she. Slowly, he brought his hand up to her left breast. She leaned into him. They stood there for a while, no longer kissing, just upright with Nigel's hand on her left breast.

Then he said, "Is this really happening?"

"Ay Dios."

"I just need you to tell me if this is real."

"This is real," she said, then started to cry again.

Nigel took his hand off her breast and just held her until she was done.

As they walked back, Nigel became increasingly panicked that people might have noticed their absence. Voices grew louder as they neared Matthew's lawn, and much more light shone through the branches than before. Electric light. Floodlights from the garage and strings of white bulbs hung over the patio. While they'd been gone, the electricity had returned.

At the edge of the woods, where Matthew's lawn met the first pines, a frog croaked and Elena jabbed the gig at the base of a tree. Nigel heard the spear strike wood. Then she held the little trident up, backlit against the lights from the house, and Nigel saw the outline of two dangling frog legs, kicking.

Elena carried her frog around the crowd, holding it aloft like a torch. Sporadically Nigel would hear an excited yelp or moan as she moved from group to group.

Matthew's stepsister and her new husband were preparing to

leave. Nigel found Matthew at the edge of the driveway, setting down the buckets of roman candles. In the electric light, he looked pale, sweaty, and tired.

The bride was hugging a whole line of people. Her white dress had a six-inch cuff of mud around the bottom, but she didn't seem to mind. Her husband kept giving high fives and whooping with people calling him Stu-driver.

"Come on," Matthew said. "It's time to blow this stuff up."

And then Matthew was all business, distributing roman candles, winking at people, giving orders, and handing out extra-long matches. He turned off the floodlights, and as the bride and groom drove away, a bevy of roman candles lit up the sky, leaving undulating blue orbs floating across Nigel's vision.

The crowd thinned rapidly. At least one man had already thrown up on the front lawn. The grass was worn into muddy circles around the tiki lamps and the drink tables. Matthew's mother walked past Nigel on her way out and said, "Why don't you move home and leave the labels in Atlanta?"

Nigel considered what it would be like to live in Lystra again. He could see the whole town at that moment. He knew that Duke Power employees were on cherry-pickers mending power lines, and he knew how the children were disappointed that the power had returned. Dogs on walks at that very moment were finding themselves overwhelmed by objects to sniff, branches to carry, new puddles to drink from. He knew everything in Lystra. Everything. He didn't need to see it.

"Someday," Nigel said.

He went inside to avoid the rest of the departures. The kitchen was empty and he took the last deviled egg upstairs. The photo album was in the same place. The Polaroid was still there. He still wasn't in it.

He flipped back through the album. There were so many photos of him. He had played saxophone in marching band. He had gone to Michael Lipsitz's Bar Mitzvah and worn a yarmulke. He had done a handstand on someone's yellow couch. He did exist.

Nigel walked downstairs after he was sure everyone had gone. Matthew and Elena had their arms around each other on the couch. The lights were off and the room was lit by low burning candle stubs. Elena's head was nestled between Matthew's shoulder and ear.

"Baby, we're gonna go smoke," Matthew said.

Matthew kissed the top of her head, and Elena motioned softly with her hand as if to say *fine*. The gesture struck Nigel as quintessentially European.

Nigel had taken off his shoes and when he stepped onto the porch, the brick felt clammy and slick on his bare feet. There were cigarette butts strewn down the steps. Plastic champagne flutes lay scattered across the lawn, in the middle of which sat two wooden chairs from the dining room.

"Hey," Nigel said. "About earlier, I think you're right."

"About what?" Matthew said, spitting a piece of tobacco off his tongue as he lit a miniature cigar.

"Lily Vanstory."

"We really still talking about this?"

"I saw the photo and I'm just saying you were right."

Nigel stepped into the lawn. It had been years since he'd felt wet grass on his feet.

"What you need is a girl," Matthew said. "No. Listen to me. I know how your luck's been. Why don't you move home? We could have a good time. What! I'm serious. I miss you, man."

"What would I do?" Nigel said.

"You can do whatever you want. You got your shit together more than anybody I know."

Underneath one of the chairs lay the frog gig, the frog still speared on the end.

"Hey," Matthew said, picking it up. "You see this?" He bounced the frog slightly, the barbed tips extending through its side.

"That's a big frog," Nigel said.

"No shit! Elena caught it."

"Really."

"Yeah. These things get confused when the water rises," Matthew said. "They go all over the place. You ever done it?"

"Done what?"

"Frog gigging."

"No," Nigel said.

"Well, we'll go next time you're in town," Matthew said. "When you move back."

Nigel looked at the frog, its body held fast on the barbs as it bounced, the skin tight and muscular. He knew that he'd seen those frog legs alive, backlit and kicking. He knew that he'd been there, that he'd heard the spear hit wood, that he'd seen her kill it.

"Shhh," Matthew said. "Listen."

The air conditioner was running again, so they weren't as clear as they had been earlier, but a few intermittent croaks sounded loud and consistent from the woods.

"Come poke me with a spear," Matthew said. "That's what they're saying. Come get me, Nigel. Come home."

spirits

⊖   ⊖   ⊖   ⊖   ⊖   ⊖   ⊖   ⊖   ⊖

George stepped into Kenny Craven's yard and everyone quit talking. He was sweating through his mesh T-shirt, drops sliding down his expansive pocked face and glistening on his giant arms. Every neighbor there was silently looking at him, their faces lit from underneath by the undulating light of the charcoal grills. Smoke curled around the indistinct forms and their collected thawing perishables.

Parties like these always popped up after hurricanes knocked the power out. Hurricane Hugo had blown inland that morning, and though they'd only gotten the edge of it in Lystra, the power had been out for more than twelve hours now. Coolers of melting ice held everything saved from thawing refrigerators—floating bottles of champagne, eggs, Mountain Dew, beer, yogurt, ranch dressing, white wine. A card table was covered with newspaper, on top of which lay the meat. A gaping rack of ribs, steak, bacon, sweaty ground chuck, and an open baggie of translucent shrimp. Kenny was in the midst of cleaning a pile of quail carcasses, shoving plucked feathers into a plastic bag, but many of the smallest feathers continued to escape and float on the same variant air currents as the smoke, twirling and rising into the darkness. Kenny stopped plucking to look at George, and several small feathers fell back into the light. One gently settled onto his head.

"George is back," Kenny said, and everyone turned to look.

Before the accident, George had been a compulsive weightlifter —272 pounds of muscle. He hadn't lifted more than a few times since November, though. That was ten months. He had kept the weight, but it was no longer muscle. His stomach bulged under his

T-shirt, his neck stood like a ledge under his chin. He was sweating so much that he had seen more than one drop fall from his eyebrows. George lived in Durham now, but had come to town to be with his parents during the storm. This was the first time he had seen anyone in ten months. The first since he had killed Huynh Tang.

― ― ―

George hadn't caused the accident. He had simply been driving his Volvo station wagon through the intersection of Beasley and Hoover on Thanksgiving Day when Huynh Tang smashed his head through the passenger-side window, breaking most of the bones in his face, ripping flesh and hair off of his scalp and leaving much of it in the car before sliding out and landing partially under the tires that George was trying to stop. Huynh Tang was a hyperactive twelve-year-old who had been skateboarding as fast as he could downhill before running a stop sign and hitting the side of George's car. George just happened to be driving by. There were witnesses. Huynh Tang had hit George. Not the other way around. Huynh Tang had caused his own death.

― ― ―

"Yeah!" Manny yelled, approaching George. "He's back on the town and ready to Wang Chung!"

Manny's blond pompadour gleamed like molded plastic in the firelight, and his extreme features resembled those of an anatomical drawing, all sinew and lips. He was a friend of George's from high school and lived in another rental house directly across the street from Kenny. All the houses in this neighborhood looked the same—small, with unmowed lawns, gravel driveways, and concrete steps with weeds growing between cracks.

"Champagne for my real friends," Manny said, holding out a jar of champagne. "Real pain for my sham friends."

George walked away. He didn't think he could go through with this. But then Manny grabbed his shirt, pulling it so tight that a few rigid tufts of chest hair popped through the thin fabric.

"Hey, big guy," Manny said. "Wait."

George turned to Manny, but Manny wasn't looking at him. George followed his gaze. Manny was looking at Huynh Tang.

He was actually looking at Huynh Tang's older brother, but in Huynh Tang's family, everyone had the same name. George didn't know if that was part of their official naming system or not, but in Lystra, Huynh Tang was both singular and plural, like, "There's Huynh Tang," if the whole family was out, or, if you saw just one family member, "Hey, Huynh Tang. How you doing?"

Huynh Tang were Vietnamese. North Carolina had become the relocation point for a large group of Vietnamese refugees, mountain dwellers known as Montagnards. The Montagnards had served alongside American troops in the Vietnam War but had been left behind after the withdrawal. A local doctor, Sheldon May, had donated enough money for Huynh Tang to come to Lystra and start a landscaping company. With it, Huynh Tang bought a riding mower that they used for a long time as a car, slowly buzzing through neighborhoods from job to job, waving to their clients.

This Huynh Tang, the one George was looking at now, was the oldest of the two Huynh Tang boys and had been in George's high school class. They hadn't been friends, just classmates, but friendly. George hadn't seen him since before the accident.

Huynh Tang looked exactly like his younger brother. George couldn't see that face without envisioning it violated by glass and concrete. The dark eyebrows, matted with blood. The wide nose, flattened and angled onto the cheek. Dark, wiry hair, the same that had spread itself throughout his car, still attached to small clumps of flesh.

George had heard on the radio that today was the first day of fall. A new season and a storm. It felt like the right time to try to finish things, to start things. This was the reason he had come to Kenny's house. He knew Huynh Tang lived on the street and spent time with both Kenny and Manny. He knew he would see him here.

"Hi," George said.

"Hey," Huynh Tang said. His English was barely passable. "How are you?"

"OK. I'm working at Meats and Treats."

"OK."

"I have to say something."

"No. You don't have to say anything."

"No, I do, though. I came here to see you, to let you know how sorry I am. I should have said that earlier. I just—"

"No," Huynh Tang said. "I am sorry."

"Come on," George said.

"You know what my brother's been saying."

"What?"

"You've heard what my brother has been saying."

"No."

"I thought maybe you had. He has spoken to so many people, telling stories."

"Are you talking about . . . who are you talking about?"

"My younger brother."

George just looked at him.

"Our family believes in Caodism, George. Spirits. They talk to us."

"How?"

"We use a special tool called Ouija board."

"A Ouija board?"

"Yes."

"That's a fucking toy."

"No. It is Caodist tradition. My brother has been talking very much to us."

"Are you serious?"

"Yes."

"OK. I . . . haven't heard this."

"He's been saying that you drove into him. He says maybe you were drunk. Wait. He does not say this to me. He only speaks to me about love. But he says this to our mother, and many people. This is what I am sorry for."

"What the fuck are you talking about?" George said.

"No, I know. That is why I am sorry. The dead cannot admit mistakes. I know he is making stories. I am just sorry that he will not stop. So many people speak to my brother."

George looked at the neighbors gathered across the lawn. Had other people heard this?

"I gotta say, man. This just . . . this is just blowing my mind right now."

They stood in silence for a moment, and then fireworks began to explode some miles away, shimmering blobs of white low on the horizon. It must have been another hurricane party, probably in Mankin Park.

"It's a sign!" Manny yelled.

"Of what?" Kenny said.

"I don't know! But follow me!"

Suddenly people were swarming around them, laughing, passing bottles, carrying them along. Manny was leading the party across the street to his house. George knew that Manny couldn't stand spending time with Kenny—none of the neighbors could. This was a chance to move on.

At Manny's, George and Huynh Tang went inside with the crowd. There were probably twenty people packed into the small, candlelit living room alone. People were drunk, loud, full on meat, totally uninhibited. Two girls from high school were licking each other's faces. Huynh Tang began talking to their friend Bryce, who had gone completely bald since the last time George had seen him. A white pit bull was closed into the kitchen with a baby gate across the door. Manny was everywhere, giving high fives, screaming. People were holding hands, whispering in ears, and kissing.

This was when one fluorescent bar on the ceiling began to flicker to life, and George felt an improbable disappointment, the same as when one of Lystra's ephemeral snowfalls melted in the morning sunlight. The electricity was back.

Manny rushed to a huge stereo-karaoke system in the corner and turned it on, knobs and meters glowing green against the brushed aluminum.

"Let's Wang Chung!" he said.

Then he started fumbling through a shoebox of cassette tapes.

George made his way to Huynh Tang.

"Huynh Tang," he said. "It was good to see you, but I'm gonna go."

"Is there any message you would like for me to give to my brother?"

"I don't mean any disrespect, but I just don't believe in this stuff. At all. I need this to end."

"Spirits never end."

"I mean all of this. Do you even know what I'm talking about? I was really fucked up for a long time, man. I used to be a normal guy. I mean, I was shitting all over the place. Literally, like on my couch and stuff. I dropped out of college. I still can't sleep. I can't drive. I'm scared all the time. I wish it hadn't happened. That's about the most of it. I just wish I hadn't been there. I wish I had never been there. I wish it was all, just—" he waved his hand in the air.

"I can tell him that," Huynh Tang said.

"I don't mean that I want you to tell him that. I'm just telling you."

"He might have already heard."

"Look. If you really want to tell him something, tell him that I wasn't drunk. That I was just going home, man. I wasn't doing anything."

"OK."

"I was just driving."

"I know. I'll tell him."

"I mean, I wasn't even driving fast. I was just driving. Tell him, I don't know. I mean, look at me."

Huynh Tang looked at him.

"What the fuck, man?" George said. "What do you see?"

Huynh Tang didn't answer.

"I'm sorry," George said. "I didn't mean to raise my voice. You don't deserve that. I'm just—"

Then rock music came on so loud that there was no chance of hearing anything over it. Huynh Tang motioned for George to follow him outside.

The storm had blown a strange layer of branches, party detritus from Kenny's house, and neighborhood oddities across the ground. The streetlights were on now and illuminated a small toy shovel in the driveway. A pink blazer with its arms outstretched lay prostrate on a lawn. Loose paper shone like white holes in the ground. A cassette's magnetic tape was unspooled, glittering across the tar fillings on the road. An alarm was sounding from someone's house and George thought it was strange that anyone in that neighborhood would even have a house alarm.

"I want you to talk to him," Huynh Tang said.

"No."

"I live right there. Come on."

"This isn't my thing."

"I'll show you," Huynh Tang said. "Come."

Huynh Tang lived alone in a minuscule house just a few doors away. It consisted of two rooms, basically a storage shed with a bathroom.

Inside, the main room had several framed photos of him and his brother as children in Vietnam, holding machine guns in the jungle. The younger Huynh Tang was looking at George from so many different angles holding so many different guns. Huge guns. Smiling with belts of ammunition around his shoulders. He couldn't have been more than eight in those photos.

All of the furniture was made from variations of plastic and particle board. George sat in one of the plastic chairs and it sagged beneath him as Huynh Tang set up his Ouija board. It was homemade, just blue magic marker on cardboard. Capital letters arced in two rows beneath a crescent moon and a sun. The moon had NO written on it and the sun read YES. At the bottom, the words GOOD BYE stretched the length of the board below a crude drawing of a flower growing out of a pyramid.

"So, you've never done this?" Huynh Tang asked.

"Only, like, playing."

"This is not playing. Place your fingers here. Here," Huynh Tang said.

George perched his meaty fingers atop an upturned shot glass with a map of Texas printed on the side. Huynh Tang's fingers were on the opposite edge of the glass, the tips slightly touching George's.

spirits

"Just barely," Huynh Tang said.

The music from Manny's house played tiny through the open windows. The house alarm continued sounding, and George could smell his own sweat. He was embarrassed, sitting there in silence at the Ouija board, touching Huynh Tang's fingers.

Then the shot glass moved. Slightly.

I

The motion accelerated.

AMDEAD

The glass made a constant scratching sound as it slid from letter to letter, and George felt his hand being led by a force that was not his own. It was terrifying but exhilarating.

BUTIKNOWWHATYOU

George wasn't pushing it at all. He couldn't believe this. The glass continued scratching.

DID

Adrenaline rushed through his system and he felt like his fingers might begin to shake. He tried to open his soul to anything. He was ready to allow the spirit in. Quicker now, the glass spelled out the rest, jerking from letter to letter.

YOUKILLEDMYBROTHER

Then Huynh Tang took his fingers off and the glass fell to its side.

"I don't think we should go on," Huynh Tang said. "It might just get worse."

George was breathing in short gasps. Trying to take it in. You killed my brother. You killed my brother.

"Wait," George said. "But he said, 'You killed my brother.'"

"I told you."

"No. But he said that I killed his brother. You see what I'm saying? That would mean you."

George could almost see the English pronouns floating through

Huynh Tang's mind as he tried to sort out what had just been said.

"You were pushing it," George said.

"No! This is a tradition."

"I don't give a shit what it is. You just spelled that out."

Huynh Tang folded the board in half.

"If you don't believe, then it will not work."

"I believed it," George said. "I did. But I know you just did that."

"I don't know why he said 'my brother.' How can I know?" Huynh Tang said. He held his open palms to the ceiling. "I don't know what just happened. I don't know why my brother is saying these things. I am sorry for what he says."

"For what he says? That was you! What the fuck, man?"

"I just," Huynh Tang said. His face had become swollen and his eyes began filling with water. He covered them with his small dark hands and said, "At home, everyone talks to spirits."

"What does that have to do with anything?"

George listened to the alarm for a few seconds and watched Huynh Tang hold his head.

"Hey," George said. "OK. Forget about it. Let's go back to Manny's. What do you think? Let's just leave this all right here."

As George and Huynh Tang entered Manny's living room, Manny was twisting his bony hips back and forth across the carpet. The music was louder than before and he was twisting low to the ground, his pointy knees at angles from his hips. Everyone was twisting with him, following his lead. Then he rose, still twisting, and so did everyone else.

A girl who had gone to high school with them, Mandy Phelps, put her hand out in a motion like *you too*. She grabbed Huynh Tang and pulled at him. He looked awkward but started to twist with her, her drink spilling onto his shirt.

spirits

It was the song "Rock You Like a Hurricane," by the German rock band the Scorpions. George could tell that Manny had been waiting for this chance to sing a song about a hurricane during a hurricane. He held a microphone that was plugged into the stereo and sang into it as hard as he could.

"It's early morning, the sun comes out!"

Mandy Phelps grabbed George now and he felt like he couldn't just stand there, so he started twisting too. She drifted off, drunk, twisting and bumping into people until someone pushed her towards a corner, where she just twisted by herself.

Manny kept singing. *"My cat is purring, and scratches my skin!"*

Someone's drink splashed onto the side of George's face, and as the chorus started, people began to sing in unison with Manny.

"Here I am! Rock you like a hurricane!"

Huynh Tang's dark, wiry hair swung from side to side as he danced. His eyes were closed. He was not singing. He looked focused and removed and almost in a trance.

"Here I am! Rock you like a hurricane!"

The second verse started, but Manny was the only one who knew these words. A man with no hair on top of his head but a ring of long hair around the sides that was tied into a short ponytail reached out and poked Huynh Tang in the stomach. His eyes opened and met George's and they twisted in unison for a moment, until George cast his gaze downward. He twisted hard, throwing sweat from side to side. The chorus came around again and it seemed like everyone but George and Huynh Tang was singing. George didn't want to sing if Huynh Tang wasn't. He didn't want to look like he was celebrating anything.

"Here I am! Rock you like a hurricane!"

Then Manny was beside them and he pushed his microphone into Huynh Tang's hand, motioning like *come on!* Huynh Tang awkwardly put it to his lips and said, "Hello?"

His voice blasted through the speakers.

Manny smiled and gave him an enthusiastic thumbs-up. He was bringing the twist low now and people were getting down. Then he turned to George, smiling, and reached his arms around George and Huynh Tang, pulling them into a huddle. Manny smelled like smoked onions, and Huynh Tang had the microphone crammed into their faces. They were almost twisting on their knees now. George's mouth wasn't but an inch from Huynh Tang's and he could feel Huynh Tang's breath on his face, his lips, falling into his mouth. George was twisting in Manny and Huynh Tang's arms, he was smelling Huynh Tang's breath, he could feel Huynh Tang's hair swinging into his eyes and across his face. His own arm was around Huynh Tang's neck, and now Huynh Tang's lips opened and so did George's, they both sucked in air, and then it seemed like all of Lystra began to sing.

"Here I am!"

Nic Brown is a graduate of Columbia University and the Iowa Writers' Workshop. He lives with his wife and daughter in Chapel Hill, North Carolina. *Floodmarkers* is his first book.